Katie

GOD'S WONDERFUL RAILWAY:

CLEAR AHEAD

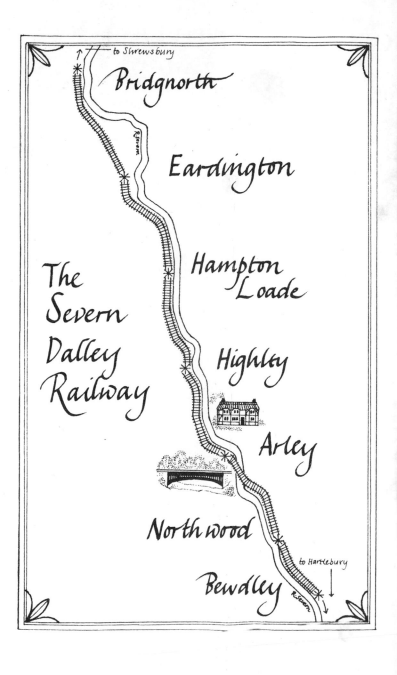

to Shrewsbury

Bridgnorth

R.Severn

Eardington

Hampton
Loade

The
Severn
Valley
Railway

Highley

Arley

Northwood

to Hartlebury

Bewdley

R.Severn

GOD'S WONDERFUL RAILWAY:

CLEAR AHEAD

Avril Rowlands

BRITISH BROADCASTING CORPORATION

To all Great Western Railwaymen
including Donald Wilden who started as
a lad porter in 1909 and whose
comments have been invaluable

This story is based on the BBC TV series
GOD'S WONDERFUL RAILWAY first shown in 1980.
It was produced by Paul Stone and
directed by John Prowse. The main characters
who appear in the book were played
as follows: George Grant, Ian Sandy; Mr Jellicoe,
Richard Pearson; Jane Grant, Shirley Cain;
Robbie Grant, John Barrett; Annie, Suzy O'Hara

Illustrated by Jo Worth

Published by the
British Broadcasting Corporation
35 Marylebone High Street
London W1M 4AA

ISBN 0 563 17828 0

First published 1980
© Avril Rowlands 1980

Printed in England by
Jolly & Barber Ltd, Rugby, Warwickshire

I

The day of his grandmother's funeral ranked in George Grant's mind as the most dreadful day in his life. As he stood in a line with the other members of his family beside his grandmother's newly dug grave in the village churchyard, he was sweating profusely, even though it was a chilly, wet, blustery sort of day.

George was both uncomfortable and unhappy. He was encased in his "best" black Sunday suit, which had seen many years of wear and now fitted him with the constraint of a strait jacket. He tried holding his breath for fear of bursting the buttons on his over-strained waistcoat, and ran his finger round the inside of his collar to ease the strangling effect it was having against his windpipe. He shifted his considerable weight from his left foot to his right and back again, until he caught sight of his mother's frown of disapproval.

There was an oppressive atmosphere in the churchyard. Although he had not known his Grandmother Deborah well, George felt an almost overwhelming sense of family history, family sadness, that pressed down on him as he stood, head bowed, listening to the service.

His great-grandfather, John Grant, was buried here in the churchyard at Arley. John Grant had been a railway navvy and had been killed in an accident at Victoria Bridge. He was something of a legend to George for he had worked on the final stages of the construction of the railway that had since provided employment for all George's relations.

George stole a glance at his grandfather. Robbie Grant was an old man with a long white beard and deep-set hawk-like eyes. He walked with a slight limp, and when he spoke, his voice carried traces of a soft, Scots accent. Robbie was standing stiffly apart from everyone at the foot of the grave. He looked like a carved statue, he was so still, and his eyes stared unseeing into space.

George was frightened of his grandfather. He was frightened of many people, but his grandfather came quite high on his list of people he was most scared of. There was no real reason for this fear except that his grandfather looked stern and was old. But George had been frightened of him as a child when his mother would threaten to tell Grandfather Robbie of George's misdeeds, and he was frightened of him now, even though George was turned fourteen and could almost be called a man.

The vicar moved forward, his surplice flapping round him like some great bird. He opened his hand and threw the first clod of earth down on the coffin. ". . . earth to earth, ashes to ashes, dust to dust; in sure and certain hope of the resurrection to eternal life, through our Lord Jesus Christ."

One by one, the men, led by Robbie, stepped forward and threw the earth they were holding down on to the coffin. George was clasping a small amount of earth in his hot, sweating hand. He had picked some up, on his mother's instructions, before the service started and had been anxiously turning and turning it over until it had become a sticky ball of clay.

George stepped forward, opened his hand, and the clay ball stuck firmly to his palm. Feverishly, with, he felt, everyone watching, he scraped away at the earth with his other hand until he heard his mother hissing, "George!" He cast an agonised glance at her, took a step backwards and slid ungracefully over the wet grass to end on his knees at the edge of the open grave.

He would never forget the shame of that moment. It far surpassed all the other clumsy and embarrassing things he had ever done. As long as he lived he would be able to recall vividly every detail: the smell of the wet earth; the Vicar pausing in mid-sentence; the sudden horrified silence broken by a hurriedly-stifled snigger from his cousin. And, above all, the dreadful, dreadful fear that one false move could send him plunging straight down into the grave on top of his grandmother's coffin.

He inched back from the grave and the service continued. Head bowed, face scarlet, trousers muddied and torn, George gave a scared sideways glance at his grandfather and suffered a further shock. George suddenly realised that his grandfather had not even noticed the awful thing he had done, and for some inexplicable reason that made it a hundred times worse.

Two weeks later George was hurrying down the street one evening with a can of tea, bound for his grandfather's signal-box at Highley Station. "And mother wants him to come and live with us," he thought despairingly.

George felt the familiar butterflies in his stomach perform their familiar war dance. It was bad enough having to deliver his mother's message, he thought, but to have to go to Highley Station to do it was just too unfair, for in one week's time George was to start work at the station in the humble post of Lad Porter.

It was not that George minded the idea of working for the

railway. That had never entered into things. He had always known that when he left school he would work for The Railway. Not for just *any* railway of course, but for the Great Western Railway which had employed members of George's family for almost forty years, ever since the Great Western had taken over the old Severn Valley Railway shortly after it opened. Now, in 1906, George was following the family tradition which had started with his grandfather. His father had been a clerk until he went off to war and was killed fighting the Boers, and his brother, his uncle and his cousin were all railwaymen.

What terrified George was not the thought of the railway, it was the thought of starting work at all. "I'm sure to do everything wrong," he said to himself, "I always do."

It was getting dark when George reached the station and he peered anxiously along the platform. There was no one to be seen, which was a relief as he had dreaded meeting any of the station staff.

The platform was quiet, neat and orderly. Some wheel-barrows were stacked against a wall with military precision; a group of empty milk churns waited in tidy rows for collection by the local farmers; large wooden crates were piled methodically in a corner. Even the plants in the strip of garden along the fence appeared well-watered, well-weeded and well-regimented, and the garden tools hung clean and polished on their appointed hooks near the water pump. George gulped. There was not a speck of dirt or dust to be seen on the freshly swept and washed-down platform – or anywhere else for that matter.

Forgetting for a moment the errand he had been sent on, George wandered along the platform and wondered what it would be like to work there as a Lad Porter. He was not very sure what a Lad Porter did, except help people with their luggage and things. He was very shy, and the prospect of approaching total strangers with offers of help was rather daunting. He wondered, too, whether he would be expected to keep the station as neat and tidy as it was now and he felt sick at the thought for he was not naturally neat or tidy.

He passed a door marked "Private" and then another marked "Stationmaster" and the sick feeling grew worse. Suppose the Stationmaster had not gone home, but was waiting behind his closed door, waiting to pounce on George and demand to know what he was doing trespassing on the railway a full week before he was due to start work there? Or suppose he was looking out from behind one of those curtained windows – which George knew was where the Stationmaster lived – and shouted down at him, "Hey boy! You, boy! Clear off!"

George looked up fearfully, but there was no irate twitching of the curtain and the Stationmaster's door remained shut. He looked across the track and remembered his errand as he saw the signalbox. Slowly he walked towards it.

The signalbox at Highley Station was situated exactly opposite the one station platform. It was a square building whose entrance was reached by a set of steps at the side. A faint glow of light showed that his grandfather was working inside. George looked back at the station building. The station might be under the rule of the Stationmaster but the signalbox – standing like some lonely, isolated fortress on the far side of the track – looked as if it were solely his grandfather's domain.

When George reached the top of the steps he looked in through the glass window before knocking on the door. He saw a room glowing with the golden light cast by an oil lamp. He saw a world on its own, a small, square world, three sides glass, which looked out on inky blackness, for by now it was quite dark outside.

Along one side were banks of levers topped by a highly polished wooden shelf with a row of brass signal bells. On another shelf sat a telephone with a train register and a well-sharpened pencil. Two large token instruments, used in single-line working, stood against a wall. The floor had been scrubbed and polished until it gleamed, and light glinted off the brass and polished wood. It was a warm room, a friendly room. A cheerful fire crackled in the well-leaded grate, and before it sat a figure huddled in an old armchair.

The figure moved slightly and George could see his face clearly. George's heart suddenly began to thud. His grandfather looked as if he were in pain. But – no, it was not pain. It was sadness and loneliness, such sadness and such loneliness that George was shaken as he peered in through the window.

George took a step back, feeling that he had intruded on something he should never have seen – something altogether private. In moving he knocked the can of tea against the glass and he heard his grandfather get up. The door opened and golden light flooded over George. His grandfather stood in the doorway staring down at him, looking tired and questioning, but otherwise the same as always. That dreadful expression was gone.

"T-tea Grandfather?" stammered George. "Mother sent it." He held out the can.

"Did she. That was kind." Robbie sounded distant, as if his thoughts were miles away. "Thank her from me."

He took the can and went back inside, shutting the door firmly behind him. George stood uncertainly for a moment, then turned and hurried down the steps, across the track and away from the station. He felt ashamed. Ashamed and embarrassed all at once. His cheeks burned red.

He was half-way home when he realised he had forgotten his mother's message. His mother would be furious with him. He turned and looked back at the station. He could not go back. He could not bear to face his grandfather again. He heard the distant whistle of the late-night goods train and that decided him. He would rather face his mother than go back.

2

"So you didn't ask him," his mother said, her voice sharp with annoyance, her face registering extreme disapproval.

George stood in front of her feeling very small. "No ma," he said miserably.

Jane angrily finished stitching a hem on her sewing machine and did not speak. George picked up her scissors, started to fiddle with them and was firmly rapped over the knuckles. "Oh you're a fool! I should never have sent you!"

"Shall I – shall I – go back?" George asked timidly, hoping that she would not make him.

"Don't be ridiculous," she said. "I'll go myself. Tomorrow."

The next day she dressed herself with care, put on her best coat and hat and, precise to a pin, set off for the station, borne up by her consciousness of doing the Right Thing.

She returned, an hour later, looking pleased with herself. "That's all settled then," she said, taking off her gloves and smoothing out the wrinkles.

"Is Grandfather . . . ?" asked George, who was anxiously hovering in the hall.

"Yes," she said, removing the long hat-pins from her hat. "Grandfather's agreed to come and live with us." She removed her best hat carefully and patted her hair smooth, critically staring at herself in the mirror. She caught sight of George biting his bottom lip. "Don't just stand there with that moon face of yours," she said crossly, stripping off her coat and reaching for her apron. "We've a lot to do."

The next few days were spent under the eagle eye of his mother, shifting heavy furniture, scrubbing, cleaning and polishing. She cleaned and scrubbed in a glow of self-righteousness and talked incessantly about "giving the poor man a home" and "doing one's Christian duty". She felt so self-righteous that she forgot to give George more than a mild scold when he broke the mirror that stood on the chest-of-drawers.

George was scared of his mother. She topped his list of people he was most scared of. He knew, he had always known, that of all the things his mother most disapproved of – and there were many – for some reason she disapproved of him most of all. His elder brother Colin had been his mother's favourite, while George had never evoked anything more maternal than a disapproving sniff. George put his mother's attitude down to his being stupid and clumsy and unlike his brother Colin in every way, but secretly he wished, just once, that he could make his mother proud of him.

Eventually everything was ready. George waited at his bedroom window, dressed once more in his hated "best" suit, and watched the cart bringing Grandfather's few bits of furniture with Grandfather himself slowly walking by the side. Suddenly George could stand it no longer. Quietly he slipped away down the stairs, out of the back door and along the lane to find his best – his only – friend and pour out all his troubles.

Ted Jarvis was a few months older than George and was a tall, well-built, popular lad. It was an unlikely friendship – for which George felt humbly grateful – which had started after Ted had defended George against a crowd of bullies in the school playground. After summarily dispersing the bullies with a few well-aimed punches, Ted had taken George's arm. "We railwaymen must stick together," he had said, for Ted was the only other boy in the class who also came from a railway family. They had been friends ever since.

Ted thought George clever – a fact which would have astonished both George and his mother had they known – and George thought Ted the epitome of everything he would like to be but was not.

This was especially true at present for Ted had left school some weeks ahead of George and could now be classed among the ranks of Working Men. For the past six weeks he had been employed by the Great Western Railway as an engine cleaner, and what amazed George was that Ted actually seemed to be *enjoying* the work.

When George finally found Ted he was given no opportunity to pour out his troubles for Ted was hopping with excitement and swept George off in the direction of the railway.

"Come on, shift yourself, George!" Ted commanded, and he raced off up a steep flight of steps that led to a farm crossing over the track.

George followed more slowly. He heard a distant whistle, and Ted turned. "We'll miss it!" he yelled. "Come *on* George!"

When George eventually reached the crossing he saw a train rapidly approaching and Ted dancing about at the side of the track. It was the usual branch line train, a small, green tank engine pulling three coaches and a cattle truck. George could not see anything special to get excited about.

The engine whistled a warning and Ted raised his hand in a

most professional-looking way as acknowledgment. Then, as the train thundered past them, Ted pulled off his cap and waved it excitedly at the small figure of the driver. The driver grinned broadly and waved back.

"It *is* dad driving! I *told* you!" Ted said ecstatically, his eyes alight, waving for all he was worth.

Ted's father leant out of the passing train and waved back, as did one or two people in the carriages. Then the train swept on round a curve and out of sight. Ted sighed in satisfaction.

"I said he'd be driving today," he said, turning to George. "He's been on goods all week but I guessed it would be today. First time as driver of a passenger train . . . that'll be *me* some day. . . ."

They walked slowly back to the steps. George remembered Ted saying something about his father some time ago, but events at home had swept all the details from his mind.

"Ted. . . ." George began.

Ted was not listening. "No it won't. Won't catch me on a small branch line! I'll be driving the Cities and the Saints on the Holiday Run down to Plymouth."

Ted's ambition was to drive the best, most powerful engines on the express passenger trains and six weeks as a cleaner, the bottommost rung of the ladder to achieving that ambition, had only strengthened it.

"Grandfather's come to live with us," said George.

"A top link-driver on all the express runs – that'll be me."

"He came today," George went on miserably.

"Who?" said Ted, hearing the end of what George was saying.

"Grandfather. Ma didn't like him living on his own now Gran's dead, so he's moved in with us."

Ted was interested. "Old Mr Grant?"

"Yes. Ma said it wasn't right he should have to live alone

with us having a spare room. She said it was only doing one's Christian duty to give him some warmth and home comfort now he's on his own." George stopped suddenly. The contrasting images of his grandfather's snug signalbox and the cheerless parlour at home rose in his mind. He felt confused. "Ma said he doesn't look after himself properly – doesn't eat or take care of himself."

Ted was not attending to any of this. "He's a good man," he said firmly and George looked at him in amazement. "He tells some great stories down The Great Western when he's had a few. He can remember the very first train running." Ted spoke in a reverent voice. "Three engines and twenty-one coaches, he told me so himself."

George did not speak for a moment. His mother and Ted seemed to have a very different idea of his grandfather both from himself and from each other. It was as if they were talking about three different people.

"He's a bit . . ." George said finally. "Well . . . truth is, I'm a bit . . ." It was difficult to explain. "He looks very stern," he finished lamely.

"You wouldn't look exactly cheerful if your missis had just died," Ted replied.

"No," George said doubtfully, "I suppose not."

They crossed the field and walked along the riverbank. It had been raining and George remembered to step carefully over the puddles in deference both to his mother and to his "best" trousers.

"Come home with us," Ted urged suddenly. "We're having muffins for tea 'cos of dad."

There was nothing George would have liked better. He always enjoyed tea among Ted's warm, friendly family with his hordes of brothers and sisters.

"No – I – I'd better get back," he said regretfully.

"Suit yourself," Ted shrugged. Then he laughed. "If you think your granfer looks stern, wait till you meet old Jelly."

"Jelly?" George said anxiously.

"Jellicoe. Mr Jellicoe. Stationmaster of Highley," Ted explained patiently. "You're starting work there, aren't you?"

"Yes."

Ted gave him a sidelong look. "He eats lad porters alive from what I've heard," he said solemnly.

"Really?" George's mouth felt dry.

"Proper monster." Ted shook his head. "I wouldn't start at his station for anything."

He looked once more at George's stricken face then roared with laughter, doubling over as if in pain. "Your face!" he choked. He threw an imaginary punch at George. "You want to give old Jelly a good hiding if he's any trouble."

Ted made as if to punch him again and George recoiled, lost his balance, and slipped into a puddle. When he picked himself up he looked down at his muddied trousers. "Ma'll kill me," he said.

The parlour where Jane and Robbie sat was a sombre, forbidding room, stuffed with dark, well-polished furniture, hard chairs, potted plants, ornaments sitting primly on little lace mats, photographs in silver frames, an ornate clock and a large piano that had not been played for many years.

The table was laid with a lavish tea. There were three varieties of sandwich, fruit and sponge cake, and jam, honey and butter, all spread out on the best china tea-service.

Jane and Robbie sat at opposite ends of the table and there was an empty place between them where George should have been. Jane's eyes were grim, her mouth a thin cold line and her habitual expression of disapproval more marked than ever. She had taken no more than one small bite from one small sandwich.

At the other end of the table Robbie did full justice to the tea, slowly eating his way through the sandwiches and cake, the jam and the honey. His eyes were firmly fixed on the heaped-up plate in front of him.

"I can't imagine where he's gone," Jane said for the fourth time as the clock struck five. "I do apologise, Father." Robbie glanced up at her but did not stop eating. "It's so discourteous to you not to be here on your first day with us!"

Robbie paused in mid-bite to shrug slightly. "No matter. Lads his age . . ."

"He's a very thoughtless boy," Jane continued relentlessly. "He always has been. A most difficult child to bring up. So unlike his brother." She reached for the teapot. "What George needs, of course, is discipline," she said as she poured. "A father's discipline. Tea?"

"Oh – aye. Thank you."

"After all, he was only a baby when James got himself killed."

There was a sudden chill silence and the words seemed to hang in the air. James . . . Jane's husband, had been killed fighting in Africa. Jamie . . . who was Robbie's only son. Robbie took the cup of tea and thoughtfully stirred in some sugar.

"Let's hope George improves when he starts work," Jane continued, and glanced yet again at the clock.

"There's no harm in the lad from the little I've seen of him," said Robbie somewhat diffidently.

Jane laughed shortly. "There's not much of anything in him unfortunately. I must say I'm surprised at the Company taking him on. I suppose that was your influence."

"I had no hand in it," said Robbie.

"Well, I'm sure I don't know how he got the job then," Jane went on crossly. "It can't be on his own merits. I mean – just look at him!"

The back door banged and Jane froze in her seat. Slow, ponderous steps were heard down the hall, the parlour door handle turned and the door was pushed hesitantly open.

George, red-faced and unlovely, poked his head in. "I'm sorry I'm late," he mumbled.

Jane put down her teacup with studied calm. "Is that all you have to say?" she said in a dangerously quiet voice.

"Well. . . ."

George sidled slowly from the shelter of the door to his place at the table. Jane's eyes went from his face down past his torn jacket to his muddy trousers. "I suppose I'm expected to clean that mud off and repair your jacket?" she said in an arctic voice.

George did not reply. What was the use? As he sat he knocked against the table and the china rattled. That started a torrent of anger from his mother and he sat meekly, head bowed, wishing it would end so that he could have something to eat. He was ravenously hungry.

After a minute or two Jane suddenly remembered Robbie, sitting quietly eating at the far end of the table. "Your grandfather is here," she said, making it sound like an accusation.

"Good – good evening," stammered George.

"What he must think of you, the Lord knows!"

George's eyes were hungrily fastened on the plate of sandwiches nearest him and he put out a tentative hand.

"Oh no you don't, my lad," Jane snapped. "No tea for you until you can show your grandfather that you know how to look like a civilised human being! You can just go and get changed and wash your hands and face!"

"Yes Ma," George stood up and once more knocked against the table. "Sorry," he said.

"Don't forget to comb your hair!" echoed down the hall as he made his escape to his bedroom. He closed his bedroom door and sat down on the bed.

It was not fair, he thought, it was just not fair!

3

George lay in bed watching the first grey streaks of dawn slowly widen and brighten in the sky. Bit by bit the objects in his room took shape. The wardrobe, the chest-of-drawers with the basin and jug on top, the foot of his bed. It was quiet and still. A solitary cart trundled by in the street.

"George. George! It's five o'clock! Time you were up!"

His mother's voice shouted up at him from the foot of the stairs. He did not stir. She climbed the stairs and knocked loudly on his door. "*George!* Do you want to be late your first morning? *Get up!*"

George sighed deeply. "Yes Ma. I'm up," he called out, and he heard her footsteps receding downstairs. He remained where he was for a few moments then pulled aside the bedspread. He was fully dressed, and had been for hours. He went to the window.

It was light enough now to see the street below and George was surprised at the number of people already up and about. Farmer Jones was talking to Mrs Honeycoat; a girl hurried into a house and closed the door with a bang and some miners with their lamps, tin food boxes and grey, dirt-embedded faces were walking to the collieries. George leaned farther out. A man with a pretty girl beside him stopped on the corner and kissed. . . .

"*George!*"

George trailed downstairs and found Jane busily cutting up bread. "Your grandfather's gone," she said, and went over to the kitchen range where a pot was gently steaming. "Here's your porridge." She filled a bowl and handed it to him. "Careful now, it's hot."

George sat down with the steaming bowl and stirred the porridge slowly. For the first time in his life he was not hungry. He glanced at his mother, gingerly ate a bit, then put his spoon down. "I don't want any more," he said.

Jane looked at him. "Eat it up and don't be foolish."

"I don't want to be late."

"You've plenty of time," she replied tartly. "You've still got to feed the chickens before you go anyhow. You can't expect to shirk your jobs here just because you're working! I'm sure your grandfather will explain to Mr Jellicoe if you're a little late."

George looked at his mother and decided not to say anything. How could he ever explain the utter impossibility of arriving late on his first day? He ate as much of the porridge as he could and got up. Jane was waiting by the door with some bread done up in a handkerchief.

"There's your lunch," she said, handing it to him. "Let's have a look at you." She looked critically up and down. "Hmm." She adjusted his tie and straightened his cap. "You'll do, I suppose. Well, work hard, do what Mr Jellicoe tells you and *try* not to make a fool of yourself."

"No Ma."

As he went out Jane called after him. "And don't forget the chickens!"

The chickens had a poor breakfast that morning and protested loudly as George flung handfuls of meal hurriedly round the yard. Their protests brought Jane to the back door. "George! You'll stop them laying!" she called.

It was not a good start to his first day as a Working Man George thought, as he hurried down the village street. And he had had such good intentions as he lay in bed that morning watching the dawn rise. He was not going to be clumsy or slow or stupid and he was not going to be frightened of anything or anyone – even the formidable Mr Jellicoe.

By now the street was full of people: sleepy, serious, working people, intent on their own business. Miners going to the collieries at Kinlet, Highley and Billingsley; village girls on their way to the carpet factories and mills at Kidderminster; farmers going to market – and George going to work for the first time.

George felt a fraud among these adult people. He felt they would laugh at him if they knew, like the girls who lived next door who laughed at him and made up silly skipping songs as he passed them in the street. One such rhyme formed in his head to the rhythm of his footsteps.

> "Georgy – Porgy – Puddingy – Pie,
> Late for work, oh dear, oh my.
> Jelly'll eat you bye and bye
> Georgy – Porgy – Puddingy – Pie."

He could not get it out of his mind, and as he hurried faster and faster the words pounded in his brain: "Jelly'll eat you, Jelly'll eat you. . . ." He broke into a run down the hill to the station.

Highley Station had turned out in force and was ready to welcome its newest, its most humble, servant. The station staff stood in a well-regimented row along the platform awaiting their early-morning inspection, one of Mr Jellicoe's many innovations. They stood in the cold morning wind braving the stares of the passengers, the good-natured jokes of the mill girls and the ruder jokes of the farmers.

Suddenly from the Stationmaster's office a man emerged. Albert Arthur Jellicoe, Stationmaster of Highley, a small, self-important man, immaculately dressed from his impressive gold-braided Stationmaster's hat sitting upon his neatly trimmed grey hair down to his well-creased trousers and shining shoes.

Mr Jellicoe was a man who lived, breathed, ate and slept his job. He was very aware – and made everyone else equally aware – of the dignity of his position, but a Stationmaster's job could be a very harassing one and Mr Jellicoe was a very harassed stationmaster.

He was meticulous in the execution of his duties: he held the Rule Book of the Great Western Railway to be his Bible, and his zealous devotion to the Company was only equalled by his hatred both of the paperwork that showered down on him from Headquarters and by the trains themselves which interrupted the organised life of the station and dirtied the brilliant white line along the edge of the platform. The passengers he tolerated.

For Mr Jellicoe, life was a losing battle to uphold his standards against all the forces which daily threatened him. He nursed a secret ambition – an ambition to be Stationmaster of the station that won the Great Western's "Best Kept Station" award. Then there would be an article, and maybe even his photograph as well, in the Great Western Railway Magazine.

Every year Highley Station was entered for the award, and every year it was highly commended, while the First, Second and Third prizes went elsewhere.

Highley was a busy country station serving a mining community. With three coal-mines in the area the station was always full of coal trucks, pit props and other paraphernalia of the mines, and thus could never look as neat, as attractive and as orderly as Mr Jellicoe desired and the rules of the competition laid down.

It was a sad blow to Mr Jellicoe, but he made the best of it by running his station like clockwork and terrorising his staff. As he emerged from his office his staff straightened their respective backs, but Mr Jellicoe was not attending to them. He was staring down at his watch with a gathering frown of annoyance. He looked along the platform and at that moment George, red-faced and panting, ran up.

"Grant, is it?" Mr Jellicoe did not waste his words nor did he wait for a reply. "I'm glad to see you are punctual." He paused, and glanced once more at his watch. "Just." He clicked his watch shut and put it away in his waistcoat pocket. "My name is Jellicoe," he went on, taking in every detail of George's appearance. George felt instantly that he should have scrubbed harder at his face and polished his shoes better. "I am the Stationmaster. Has Headquarters measured you for a uniform?"

"N–no . . . sir." George stuttered with nerves.

Mr Jellicoe tutted in annoyance. "What is Headquarters about?" he said, but an answer was obviously not expected because none was volunteered.

Mr Jellicoe then clicked his fingers. "Davies. See about getting Grant's measurements."

A stooping, grey-haired man stared impassively at George's rotund form. "Right, Mr Jellicoe," he said.

"You have had a medical examination and an eye test I suppose?" said Mr Jellicoe as if he fully expected Headquarters to have erred there as well.

George nodded. "Yes sir. I went to Worcester for it."

"Davies. Find an armband for Grant to wear."

With a flourish Mr Davies produced one. "I have one here Mr Jellicoe," he said.

Mr Jellicoe took the armband and slid it up George's arm. George squinted down at it. It said "Great Western Railway" in red lettering, curved in an oval. The bottom of the oval said "Porter".

"Right, Grant," Mr Jellicoe said. "I have called my staff here to be introduced to you."

He walked down the upright line and recited each man's name as he passed. George walked with him, then wondered if he was meant to, or whether he should have stayed where he was.

"Mr Davies, Head Clerk, Mr Holmes, Head Porter, Mr Fry, Under-Clerk, Mr Harvey, Porter and Relief Signalman and Mr Wrighton, Shunter." Each man nodded or grunted as his name was called. Mr Jellicoe stopped walking and turned to George. "Then there is of course your grandfather, who is Signalman, and Mr Mason, occasional drayman, who is delivering in the village. You will take your orders from myself and Mr Holmes." Mr Jellicoe stopped for a fraction of a second, then continued in the same voice, while still staring at George: "Fry, your tie is crooked."

George dared not look round at Mr Fry. Mr Jellicoe turned to face his audience, for by now not only were the station staff lined up, but the passengers, too, were standing close by in lively appreciation of his performance.

Mr Jellicoe took out his watch once more. "Right, gentlemen, you may go about the Company's business," he said. "The six o'clock is almost due."

4

The station staff dispersed in all directions as if by magic. There was a whistle from the approaching train and the whole station became alive with bustling expectancy.

Mr Jellicoe looked at George. "Grant, you stay here," he said. "I'll see to you after the train has gone."

For George, that first train of the day was a revelation. He felt that he was standing on the platform watching a train arrive for the very first time in his life. It was an odd feeling. He had stood on this same platform waiting for trains countless times. Well, enough times anyway for the novelty to have worn off. Trains were nothing new to George. Coming as he did from a railway family, George could remember talk of railways almost from his cradle – today was different.

He stood on the platform, wide-eyed and quaking. He had a hard job to stop his teeth from chattering, from nerves, not cold, and the armband proclaiming him to be a part of all this, a Company servant, grew hot and tight around his arm.

Suppose somebody spoke to him, asked him something? The awful prospect made him feel sick.

But for the moment all eyes were on the approaching train. Rigid with tension, George found himself acutely aware of everything happening round him. Colours stood out vividly. The green of the engine contrasted with the chocolate and cream of the carriages. The copper-coloured chimney emitted thin spirals of white steam. The coal was piled high on the bunker and he could see the sudden flash of red flames as the firebox door was opened. Then he noticed for the first time how the daylight seemed suddenly cut off as the train gently ran along the curved platform. The long, thin station was turned into a tunnel with the train making a fourth side opposite the station building. The canopy that jutted out over the platform formed the roof.

The engine passed him, dripping water and smelling of steam engines – the hot, moist smell of coal dust, oil and steam.

On the platform there was a movement towards the still-moving train, and carriage doors were already being opened when the train finally stopped with a loud squeak and a sigh.

Miners spilled out on to the platform and George was pushed and jostled both by those getting off and those waiting to get on to the train. There was talking and laughing, shouting and swearing, and over all the strident voice of Mr Holmes loudly calling: "Highley Station! Highley!"

Mr Holmes and Mr Harvey bustled about, here, there and everywhere: assisting a lady to alight from the First Class; unloading crates; loading chickens; deftly manipulating heavy barrows, weaving in and out of the passengers with practised ease; unloading more crates and what looked like a feather bed; answering questions; hurrying people along; smiling, talking, closing doors; pushing the laughing, protesting girls on to the train; hurrying people along more firmly.

Everything they did was fast, business-like and slightly, just slightly, exaggerated. George felt that, despite their industry, they were watching him all the time, sizing him up and finding him very much wanting.

A First Class gentleman emerged. A gentleman with a gold-topped stick and a haughty expression. He stared at George and lifted one eyebrow, then looked down at the luggage at his feet. George felt himself shrivel up inside and looked away from him, pretending he had not seen. Mr Holmes rushed past and George thankfully saw him carry the luggage off the platform.

George was overwhelmed. He could never, ever, become part of this busy scene, importantly helping gentlemen with gold-topped sticks, going about his business, knowing what his business was meant to be and doing it without making a terrible, awful mess.

It was all over in a few minutes. The engine had been uncoupled, had run back down the length of the train on the far track and been coupled up at the other end for its journey back to Kidderminster. Mr Holmes returned to the platform and he and the guard chased the latecomers on to the train before shutting the doors firmly behind them.

Mr Jellicoe, who had been frowning at his watch for the last few seconds, gave the "right away" to the guard – the signal that the train could depart – and the guard blew his whistle and waved his green flag. With an answering whistle from the engine, the train departed – back up the line to Kidderminster.

George also felt like departing. He felt like departing for home, anywhere, so long as it was away from this dreadful station, this frightening job and this terrifying stationmaster.

Mr Jellicoe bore down on him. "Come with me Grant," he said. "This way." George found himself meekly following Mr Jellicoe off the platform and into the Stationmaster's Office.

Mr Jellicoe's office was clean, neat and tidy. It was so clean that George felt he really ought to remove his shoes as well as his cap before entering.

There was not a speck of dust to be seen or a paper out of place. True, the old but well-polished desk was piled high with memoranda, notes, rosters, registers and other paperwork, but every piece of paper was carefully and precisely placed in the neatest piles under the appropriate paperweight.

Mr Jellicoe sat himself behind his desk and beckoned George forward. He then sat back in his chair, cleared his throat and began: "There isn't a great deal I wish to say to you just at present, Grant. This is a busy station, and no doubt it will take you a day or two to accustom yourself to the way things operate. Keep your wits about you, do every task thoroughly, methodically and willingly and you won't go far wrong." He paused to allow his words to sink in.

"The Great Western Railway Company sets high standards," he said, then, opening his desk drawer, he took out a small book. It was covered in green leather and had the Great Western crest stamped on the front in gold. "Here is a copy of the Rule Book. It is for you to keep." George nervously wiped his clammy hands on his trousers before taking it.

"If you wish to progress in the service of the Company I would advise you to make a diligent study of it." Mr Jellicoe stopped and looked fixedly at George.

"Yes, sir," George replied fervently.

"Note especially the rules relating to safety," Mr Jellicoe continued. "This railway and this station in particular has always had an excellent safety record. I would be most annoyed if anything occurred to mar it. Even the smallest mishap requires a detailed report to be made out in triplicate." He paused: "I trust I make myself clear?"

"Oh, yes sir."

"No need to call me sir, Grant," Mr Jellicoe said. "Mr Jellicoe will do."

"Yes, s-er, Mr Jellicoe."

Mr Jellicoe picked up a piece of paper which lay in front of him. "Here is a list of your duties," he said. "I will explain them to you in detail. . . ."

As Mr Jellicoe read down the list, George's heart sank into his well-polished shoes. The list was endless, and as Mr Jellicoe prefixed each item with: "And this is important, Grant," or, "Note this especially well, Grant," or even: "This is a serious item, Grant," George was left with the feeling that any error on his part would be verging on the criminal. Everything was important; everything was serious; everything was confusing.

His first task that morning was to sweep the station. Mr Jellicoe told him where the brooms were kept and George managed to find them without having to ask further. He felt quite pleased with himself, and started sweeping the platform with gusto, driving a cloud of dirt and dust before him. It was a soothing job and George's spirits rose. There was nothing very difficult about sweeping after all!

But before he had progressed very far, a red-faced, angry Mr Jellicoe came towards him, a watering can in his hand. "Not like that Grant, not like that! Heavens above, have you never swept anything before?"

George was perplexed. There was only one way to sweep, surely?

"Damp it down, Grant," Mr Jellicoe explained in an exasperated voice. "You must lay the dust. I've already had one complaint from a passenger about dirt and dust flying everywhere!"

George's spirits never rose again that week as one disaster followed another.

"The lavatories must be cleaned out daily and disinfected," was next on Mr Jellicoe's list. George coped with the Gentlemen's well enough, but did not know how to begin on the Ladies Room.

He stood outside, staring forlornly at the closed door, trying to count the ladies who entered with the ladies who came out until he could be sure no one was inside.

Mr Holmes saw what he was doing and laughed. "Wouldn't stand there too long, Grant," he said. "Some of the ladies might not like it."

George turned pink. "Please, Mr Holmes, how do I know when there's no one inside?"

"You knock on the door lad, and call out."

"Call out what?"

"What you like. Use your noddle, Grant." And Mr Holmes went off to unload Mr Mason's cart.

George knocked timidly at the door and followed it up by a discreet cough. Receiving no reply he opened the door and went in. The two ladies within were not pleased. Neither was Mr Jellicoe.

"The oil lamps and signal lamps must be cleaned and trimmed every day." That was next on Mr Jellicoe's list, and George took especial care with his first lamp. He carefully positioned the ladder under the oil lamp in the waiting room. He carefully climbed it, holding the oil can at arm's length. When he reached the top he put the can down, still very carefully. Frowning with concentration he examined the lamp. The wick needed trimming so George trimmed it, cleaned it and reached for the oil can to fill it. The oil can slipped out of his grasp and fell crashing to the floor with a loud bang which startled the solitary gentleman reading his morning paper.

Oil splattered out everywhere. The hatch leading to the ticket office flew up and George could see Mr Jellicoe staring balefully out at him.

He spent most of that morning clearing up the mess, and after the incident Mr Jellicoe followed George around with the persistence of a bloodhound.

George quickly found out that Mr Jellicoe was obsessive

about cleanliness. "The buildings must be kept spotlessly clean," he impressed on George. "I want to be able to eat a meal off any part of them." He ran his finger along a ledge George had just dusted. "Not good enough, Grant," he said.

The cattle pens belonging to the station were also George's responsibility. They had to be kept scrupulously clean and replenished with fresh straw. George had to feed and water any animals and generally keep his eye on them.

Another daily chore was to pump up all the water the station needed for the day. The hand rotary pump was a fairly eccentric piece of equipment which did not take kindly to George's heavy handling and rewarded him with a fine soaking.

None of the machinery behaved properly with George. Mr Jellicoe initiated him into the mysteries of the sweetmeat machine and showed him how to release the cash drawer. It looked so easy when Mr Jellicoe unlocked it, but when George tried, he found the lock stiff, wrenched too hard and sent the entire contents of the drawer cascading across the platform, much to the delight of two small boys. He spent the next hour on hands and knees retrieving pennies from the most unlikely places.

Then there was the unfortunate incident with the weighing machine. After managing to jam its works, George was forbidden to touch it.

On his second morning, George was handed a number of posters and a pot of paste. His job was to "keep the posters, signs and advertisements up to date and undefaced", as Mr Jellicoe had instructed.

He unrolled the posters. The first one advertised "The Cornish Riviera" and there was a picture of blue sea and golden sand. George studied it. He had never been to the sea. "Fast Trains from All Parts" George read, and he wondered fleetingly what it would be like to get on a train at Highley Station and end up beside the sea somewhere.

He turned the poster on to its face and slapped paste over the back, then he stuck it up on the board. Mr Fry came past. "T'aint square, young Grant," said Mr Fry, putting his head on one side to view it better. "Better not let Jelly see it like that."

George stripped it off and started again.

The last item on Mr Jellicoe's list read: "To assist generally, as and when required." George found that that covered anything and everything. To start with it meant helping to handle all the goods traffic, for the railway provided the link with the outside world.

Everything went by train. There were the daily milk churns for a start, dozens of them, deposited every morning by the local farmers. When full they were very heavy. They had to be dealt with quickly and kept out of the sun. Then there was the farm produce. There were truck loads of animals, cattle, sheep, pigs, even horses. There was timber from the forest as well as animal hides, skins and pelts. There was an enormous variety of incoming goods ranging from supplies for the local shops, beer for the local pubs, interesting looking hampers for the big house and a whole miscellany of smaller items for the people who lived in the village, as well as the daily papers, the weekly periodicals and the magazines. Whatever it was, George was involved in handling it, from truck to barrow and barrow to train and vice versa.

Another job entrusted to George was the disposal of old paper. This did not mean throwing it away – oh no! Standing instructions were very clear on that point, as Mr Jellicoe explained at length to George. All the used tickets had to be returned to Paddington station, and the receipts, invoices, waybills, notes, instructions and memoranda had to be carefully sorted, bundled, tied with string, and labelled "Stores Department, Swindon," before being entrusted to the guard of the next "up" train.

George was on his feet all day, running from one end of the

station to the other, constantly being called for by Mr Jellicoe, Mr Holmes and Mr Harvey. Somehow he muddled through each day, and each evening he was so tired that he went early to bed, only to toss and turn throughout the night dreaming of terrible mistakes he was about to make. His only consolation that first week was that he saw next to nothing of his grandfather.

But above all this, above all the various jobs he was expected to perform, lurked his biggest fear. George was terrified of meeting and dealing with the public.

"You are a servant of the Great Western Railway Company, Grant. As such you represent the Company in all your dealings with the public," Mr Jellicoe had lectured. "You must never be discourteous, abrupt, or in any way offend them. You must never ask, or expect to receive, any remuneration from passengers for the services you perform. Neither must you chatter unnecessarily or be over-familiar in your dealings with them."

George had not the slightest intention of doing either. The first time he was approached by one of the dreaded public he turned bright red and stuttered so badly that the man thought he must be ill.

The second time he was approached was when a lady leaned out of a carriage window and demanded to know why her foot-warmer was no longer warm. George was so scared he bolted up the platform and hid in the lavatory until the train had safely departed. He emerged feeling very ashamed of himself.

The third time was when Mr Holmes summoned him to carry a gentleman's case and George not only tripped over the case, he also banged the gentleman's legs with it and earned himself a stern rebuke. He felt he would never be able to approach the public in the way Mr Holmes and Mr Harvey did, saying cheerfully, "Carry your bags, sir?"

But by the end of that first week, almost without realising,

George had somehow gained enough confidence to carry a lady's luggage off the plaform and into a waiting carriage without disgracing himself. The lady smiled graciously at him and slipped something cold and hard into the palm of his hand. When George was back on the platform he looked at what she had given him. It was a threepenny piece. A whole, bright, shiny, threepenny piece! He could not believe it.

Mr Holmes watched him, amused, and called out: "First fluffings eh, Grant?"

"What?"

"Tip. First tip, isn't it?"

"Oh. Oh yes. It is."

Holmes walked off, shaking his head. "You haven't half got a lot to learn," he said.

By the end of the first week, George was exhausted. It was a relief to stretch himself out on a bank next to a railway siding where Ted was still hard at work. Not that he could see anything of Ted though, who was inside the firebox of an engine, raking out the ashes of the fire.

"How's it going then?" Ted's disembodied voice came out, from the heart of the engine.

George closed his eyes. "It's – confusing," he said. "And it's hard work." A laugh echoed through the engine. "Harder than I thought," George went on. "Much harder." He sighed. "I don't know – all I do is clean, dust, scrub, polish. All day. All the time."

There was another laugh and the raking noise stopped. Ted's head appeared over the edge of the cab, black with coal dust. "Lay you odds this engine's dirtier than your station," he said, then his head disappeared and the raking started again.

"I don't seem to be learning much about being a porter,"

said George. "I thought it was about helping people. On and off trains and with their luggage and things. Not that I'm much good at that," he added gloomily, but then brightened. "I did get my first fluffings though. A lady gave me threepence for carrying her case."

Ted's head appeared again. "Threepence!" he said incredulously. "All I ever get is a kick up the backside if I haven't done the job properly. You don't know when you're well off." He disappeared once more.

"I'll split it with you if you like . . ." George offered.

This time Ted emerged completely from the engine. As he climbed down from the cab he was grinning broadly. "Now you're talking," he said. "Come on down The Great Western and I'll tell you how to get yourself appointed Assistant Stationmaster over Reginald Davies."

"I – I'd better get home," George said uncomfortably. "Ma's expecting . . ."

Ted put his arm round George's shoulders. "Listen," he said, "you're a working man now – you've got to start acting like one."

George sighed. Why was everything so difficult, he thought. "She – gets so cross," he said haltingly. "She . . . she . . . scares me."

He thought Ted would laugh at him. Whoever heard of a fourteen-year-old working-man being scared of his mother? But no. Ted glanced at George's worried face and replied seriously: "She scares me too. And I mean it. Come on. Just a quick one."

George hesitated for a moment, then gave a tight, anxious smile. "All right," he said.

The Great Western was full of railwaymen. George looked round the crowded room, saw his grandfather in a corner and tugged at Ted's sleeve, meaning to say he had changed his mind and was off home. Ted ignored him, bought two half pints and shepherded George to a spare bench.

"How are the lads at the station?" Ted asked, as George took his first cautious sip of beer. "Played any tricks on you?"

George pulled a face, for the drink tasted bitter. "Tricks?" he asked.

"They must have done something. Everyone plays tricks on new lads."

George shook his head and took another sip.

"They shut *me* in the firebox," Ted boasted. "Shut me in and went off to tea. It wasn't half hot in there, too."

"What did you do?" George asked, horrified.

Ted shrugged. "Not much I could do. I stayed quiet for a bit until I heard Driver Wilson telling his fireman to light up the tankie. That scared me all right. Didn't fancy the thought of being roasted alive, so I started hollering."

"What happened?"

"Nothing much. They let me out after a bit. They always do something to new lads. Well, us enginemen do." He grinned. "Have to think up something for the lad starting next week," he said.

No tricks were played on George, none that he was aware of anyway. Whether that was because he did enough foolish things on his own count or because station staff were above such things, George never discovered.

He started to get to know the rest of the staff and they began to accept him enough to speak to him, occasionally. Very early on Mr Holmes, who was big and burly and had an excellent opinion of himself, took George in hand.

They were having tea one afternoon, sitting on upturned crates inside the shed. There was Mr Holmes, Mr Harvey, Mr Wrighton, Mr Mason and George. George had just made the tea and was handing it round. "You taken tea to Mr Davies, Grant?" Mr Holmes asked as he ladled sugar liberally into his cup.

"Yes Mr Holmes," George replied.

"An important man, our Head Clerk," said Mr Holmes. "Remember that."

George nodded.

"Now listen, youngster. You're old Mr Grant's grandson, right."

"Yes."

"Now Mr Grant is a fine man – a very fine man – I don't think anyone here would dispute that?" Mr Holmes waited until the murmurs of agreement had died down. "However, there must be no going to him with tales or blabbing out of turn. Got it?"

"I wouldn't," said George fervently.

"No. Well, just a friendly word of advice lad," said Mr Holmes. "We're a happy bunch here, so you do your job, keep your mouth shut and your nose clean and you'll do fine. Understand?"

George understood, and from then on he was careful not to annoy Mr Holmes.

Alfred Holmes had worked at Highley Station for a number of years and had arranged a fairly comfortable existence for himself. It was swiftly made clear to George that the First Class passengers, because of their generosity with tips, were Mr Holmes's own special province, and George might only approach them by permission.

Holmes would sometimes disappear for half an hour or so and, on his return, there would be a strong smell of beer about him, a broad smile on his face, and a hare or brace of pheasant tucked under his arm.

George knew that it was strictly forbidden for staff to leave the station without permission when on duty, but he was far too frightened of Mr Holmes, and far too aware of his own humble position to do more than wonder about these strange excursions. "Business, my lad, business," Mr Holmes had said to George after one of these visits, and George was content to believe him.

Arthur Harvey, the Porter and Relief Signalman, was a much more approachable person. He thought everything George did was a great joke and even, occasionally, explained things to him.

Reginald Davies, the Head Clerk, was an elderly, grey-haired man, worn down by his job, his wife and his thirteen children. He spent the greater part of each day in the darker recesses of the Booking Office checking and re-checking his own work and that of his Under-Clerk, Jonas Fry.

Fry was round-shouldered, untidy in appearance, furtive in manner and read "penny dreadful" magazines when he should have been checking the invoices for the inward and outward goods. Every time Mr Jellicoe caught sight of Jonas Fry, with his lanky, unwashed hair, his crooked tie, his grubby shirt and his shiny trousers, he shuddered to the depths of his fastidious soul.

George slowly began to find out how the station operated. Everything ran very smoothly, governed by the clock, the arrival and departure of the trains, and the smooth efficiency of Mr Jellicoe.

He began to assimilate some of the more confusing language of the railway, but at the beginning everything was confusing. One of his worst mistakes was caused not by his ignorance of what was meant by "up" and "down" trains, but by rushing eagerly into doing things.

He had been told to send a crate of chickens on the next "down" passenger train. Unthinkingly he had loaded the crate on to the first train that entered the station and the chickens had ended up in Worcester, instead of Shrewsbury where they were bound. Mr Jellicoe had lectured him soundly on that occasion.

"Don't ever let me find you forgetting again, Grant. 'Up' means in the direction of London or, more particularly, in the direction of the headquarters of the Company at Paddington Station. 'Down' means anywhere away from there."

He stopped, and George was much too frightened to tell him that he already knew the difference.

"I am surprised, Grant, coming from the family you do, that you are unacquainted with railway terminology," Mr Jellicoe went on, and then proceeded to explain at length other peculiarities of the railway. ". . . a train is not an engine, and an engine by itself must not be called a train. A train is only to be called a train when it comprises an engine and rolling stock – I trust you are conversant with that term?"

George nodded, bemused, but Mr Jellicoe explained anyway.

"Rolling stock being a coach, a rake of coaches, goods wagons or a combination of any or all. It is also permissible to call rolling stock without an engine a train, provided the stock is waiting for the arrival of its engine. The last lad we had caused no end of trouble by mixing things up, and I don't want those sorts of mistakes happening again. Is that clear?"

George thought it was clear, more or less, and he never made that particular mistake again. But the following day he made a far, far worse one.

6

"Look lively Grant. Pick–up's almost due."

Holmes bustled past George with his usual air of self-importance.

"What's . . . ?" George asked, but Holmes had gone. George looked round the platform. Something was about to happen. There was an air of expectancy, of tension, and far more people were around than was usual at that time of day.

"Pick–up's coming Grant," Mr Jellicoe called over to him. "Get the barrow ready."

"Yes, Mr Jellicoe."

Even Mr Jellicoe's harassed face seemed more harassed than ever, George thought. He stopped stacking empty boxes against a wall and went off in search of a barrow. When he found one, he stood beside it wondering what he should do next and wishing someone would tell him what was going on.

Arthur Harvey ran past. "You won't be needing that Grant," he said. "Not unless you mean to cart a wagon load

41

of sheep and another of pigs one by one over to the pens!"

He went off, chuckling at his humour, leaving George more bewildered than before. Farmers and traders from the village were pouring in to the station and all the staff were out on the platform, even Mr Davies.

George's grandfather emerged from the signalbox and put his arm up. "Pick-up's just left Arley," he called across the track, and Mr Jellicoe nodded.

George walked over to Harvey, who was standing at the platform's edge straining for the first glimpse of the train. "Please . . . Mr Harvey . . . what is the pick-up?"

Harvey looked at him with astonishment. "Pick-up goods," he said, as if speaking to an idiot. George just looked blank and Mr Harvey sighed heavily. "Goods train. The 2.20 from Kidder. Thursdays is wholesale market day and the train's loaded with goods and animals. There'll be a fine old rush when she comes. Now shift yourself – here she is!"

And there was a fine old rush as the train pulled into the station. The pick-up, comprising about twenty trucks and wagons, came clanking to a halt, accompanied by bleatings, mooings and squealings from the animals inside. Some of the trucks were individually labelled with their trader's name and there was a general stampede by everyone on the platform for their goods.

The platform swiftly turned into a chaotic good-natured free for all, with the tradesmen fighting each other to get their goods unloaded first and the station staff working quickly and methodically to get the goods off the train so that it could be shunted to the cattle pens for the animals to be unloaded.

Mr Jellicoe hurried impatiently up and down the platform, snapping at everyone, for he did not enjoy pick-up days. Things became too uncontrolled for his liking.

George gazed at the scene in open-mouthed amazement and did not even notice when his barrow was whipped from him by a farmer impatient to unload half a dozen sacks of seed.

Mr Jellicoe noticed, however, and rounded on George. "What are you standing there for Grant?" he said angrily. "There's unloading to be done. Look sharp about it!"

George flushed red, looked for his barrow, could not find it and hurried to the truck nearest him. For once he moved quickly and in record time he opened the doors and moved on to the next truck. The ramps of the two trucks fell with loud thuds onto the platform and were instantly superseded by the heavy stamping of animal feet.

Sheep poured out from the first truck. Dazed, frightened, unhappy sheep, they emerged on to the platform, bleated loudly and set off stampeding after each other in panic-stricken flights up and down the platform.

From the second truck pigs emerged. Large pigs who were much less timid than the sheep. They squealed their enjoyment of freedom and rushed round and round attempting to prolong it. The platform was instantly transformed from controlled chaos into total, unimaginable, bedlam.

The farmer's sacks of seeds went flying and rained down everywhere as a fine dust. Also flying went the lettuces, the carrots, the tomatoes, the fruit and everything else that had been so carefully unloaded from the train.

The animals went everywhere – into every room, round every corner. They became stuck behind the weighing machine, wedged into the Goods Office. They hurtled into the empty boxes George had been stacking. Sheep were under everybody's feet, pigs were within everybody's grasp until elusively they slithered and twisted themselves free and rampaged off again, up the platform, down the platform, over, under, into everything.

Mr Jellicoe was white as he cornered a sheep and Mr Harvey grinned as he ran a squealing pig to earth, literally, in the station garden and triumphantly grabbed its tail.

One large pig found its way into Mr Jellicoe's office and caused havoc with the papers on his desk until dislodged, not without considerable difficulty, by Mr Holmes.

The tradespeople, seeing their precious merchandise flying through the air, rescued what they could and beat the animals off with cauliflowers, lettuces and whatever other ammunition came to hand.

Animals were on the track. They dived off the platform, they fell under the train and one or two enterprising beasts made off at full speed down the line to freedom, never to be seen again.

The engine driver pulled on the whistle once to inform everyone that the train was being unnecessarily delayed and a second time to show his displeasure at the delay, while his firemen jumped down to assist the infuriated farmers rescue pigs and sheep trapped under the driving wheels. The noise was tremendous. Curses, oaths, laughter, shrieks, all mingling with the terrified bleatings and squealings of the animals.

Robbie opened the door to his signalbox, enigmatically surveyed the scene, then retreated inside and picked up the telephone. And George? George stood in the centre of it all, rooted to the spot, frozen with horror. Mr Harvey rushed past. "I wouldn't be in your shoes young Grant," he called. "Not for anything!"

A few hours later it was as if nothing had ever happened. The station was deserted – quiet, clean and at peace. Well, almost at peace. It was nearly dark and, as Arthur Harvey slowly lit the station lamps one by one he could not help but overhear snatches of the angry voice of Mr Jellicoe rising and falling from behind the closed door of the Stationmaster's Office.

". . . train delayed for twenty minutes . . . causing disruption to the schedules throughout the remainder of the day . . . valuable customers inconvenienced . . . Mr Austin's vegetables trampled over – vegetables that were entrusted into the care of the Company . . . two fences damaged . . . station garden trampled down . . . incalculable cost . . ."

Arthur Harvey grinned appreciatively and lingered over his job but eventually the last lamp was lit and he was forced to go home. It was quite dark now except for the lights on the platform and the glimmer of light from the signalbox and the Stationmaster's Office.

Inside his office, Mr Jellicoe was pacing the floor, up and down, up and down, in the full flood of his eloquence. All his anger, all his outrage that such an occurrence should have happened at *his* station could now be expressed, and Mr Jellicoe expressed his feelings with warmth and vigour. George stood in front of his desk, cap in hand, and felt that he had never been more miserable in the whole of his life.

"I have been showered with enquiries from Headquarters – they're even sending Inspector Hunt down – as if I can't be entrusted to conduct my own enquiry – and the reports to be filled in! There'll be no sleep for me tonight," he said grimly. "Nothing – I repeat – *nothing* – like it has ever happened at any of my stations before . . . nothing. . . ." Mr Jellicoe's voice nearly cracked with emotion and he paused to regain control. "I have decided to fine you fifteen shillings," he said coldly. "To be deducted from your wages in weekly instalments."

He sat down and began rummaging through the papers on his desk. "Not the most auspicious beginning to your career, Grant," he added, as he pulled the pen and inkstand towards him.

George stood white-faced and made no effort to move.

"You may go," Mr Jellicoe said curtly and began to write.

George walked out of the office, along the platform and off the station. He did not see Robbie watching him from the signalbox window. He did not see anything clearly because he was trying to choke down the big tears that were filling his eyes and running down his nose. After all, fourteen-year-old working-men do not cry.

7

By the time George arrived home he had stopped crying and had made an attempt to wipe the worst of the tear-stains from his cheeks. He prayed that his mother would not notice anything. She would learn soon enough from his grand-father, but all George wanted to do just then was to go to bed and try to blot out the terrible events of that day.

Jane met him on the doorstep. She was peering anxiously into the night and held a tea can in her hand. "There you are, George. Late again I see! I forgot the tea for your grandfather. Will you take it to him?"

George's heart missed a beat. "Now?" he asked in an unsteady voice.

"Yes," said Jane. "You can have your tea when you get home."

"Back to the station?"

"Unless he's working somewhere else," said Jane tartly.

"Must I?" George pleaded.

"George!"

"Oh, all right."

"All right? I should think all right," Jane said crossly. "Is that how you answer Mr Jellicoe when he asks you to do something – oh all right?"

George's mother had an uncanny habit of pinpointing whatever George was feeling bad about and making him feel much, much worse. George winced, touched on the raw. "No Ma," he said.

"It's just at home then, is it?" she paused, but George did not speak. "Oh go on – the tea'll get cold while you stand there dithering."

George took the can and slowly walked off and Jane watched him go. "Just like his father," she said to herself as she went inside and closed the door.

George retraced his steps back to the station, slowly, numbly. It was odd, he thought. Odd how when things seemed as if they could not get any worse, they invariably did. Never in his worst imagining would he have dreamt of being sent back to the station to face his grandfather. What would Grandfather say? George felt cold and sick. If he was *really* unlucky he might even meet Mr Jellicoe. What a terrible thought!

Mr Jellicoe *had* said he would be up all night. "No sleep for me tonight," he had said. George thought over some more of the things Mr Jellicoe had said, and shivered.

He had been right of course. Everything Mr Jellicoe had said had been right, borne out by his mother, borne out a thousand times a day by the stupid, stupid things he did. "I'm just a clumsy, fat, fool," George thought.

He met no one at the station, but the gleam of light visible from the Stationmaster's Office showed that Mr Jellicoe was still working, trying to repair the damage George had done. Seeing that light did not make George feel any happier, and he mounted the stairs to the signalbox in the blackest despair.

Robbie must have seen him coming, for the door opened abruptly. In Robbie's hand was a sock with a needle and darning wool pushed through, but George was in no mood to notice.

"Hello," said Robbie.

"Tea, Grandfather," said George. "Ma sent it – she forgot to give it to you."

He held out the can but Robbie did not take it. "Come in a minute," he said and walked back into the room.

George shuffled over the doorstep and stood just inside the door. "Close the door lad, there's a powerful draught in here."

George closed the door, then stood with his back pressed against it, ready for instant flight.

"Put that can down and come and sit by the fire."

George put down the can and nervously looked round. It was as he remembered it, warm and snug, with a cheerful fire in the grate. A kettle was hissing loudly over the fire and a brown teapot stood warming on the hearth. A pile of socks and darning wool were scattered round.

Robbie bent down and gathered up the mending which he then stuffed at the side of his chair. When he straightened up, his face was slightly flushed. "I – I got used to doing my own mending when Deborah became ill," he said, and to George's surprise he sounded almost embarrassed. "I don't like to trouble your mother. Besides – it gives me something to do. It can get a bit lonely here at times." He sat down and looked up at George, still poised by the door. "Sit down."

George sat and there was an uneasy silence broken by the sharp staccato sound of the bell. Robbie answered it, took out a token, pulled off a signal and went out into the night.

George remained where he was, feeling the warmth from the fire spread through his whole body, relaxing him and making him suddenly very, very sleepy.

He must have dozed off for a minute, for the next thing he was aware of was his grandfather speaking. He looked up and Robbie was sitting thoughtfully puffing at his pipe.

"I saw what happened today," Robbie said. "It could have happened to anyone new to the job. I expect Albert gave you a good telling off."

George was wide awake now, flushed and nervous. He stared at his feet. "He . . . he . . . said . . . ." he began in a small voice.

"It doesn't matter what he said," Robbie interrupted. "It was a silly thing to do – and you've been punished for it and learned your lesson, I hope, and there's an end to it."

"Mr – Mr Jellicoe doesn't think so," said George, and to his dismay he felt his eyes prickling with tears.

"What? That you won't go and do it again?" Robbie smiled, but George was still staring at his feet and did not notice.

"I – I'm always doing the wrong thing – I'm stupid . . . and clumsy. . . ."

"Now this is foolishness," Robbie broke in. "Everyone's stupid and clumsy when they're doing something they've not done before. You know – before I was taken on by the Company I had to learn to read and write. A grown lad who'd been working nigh on four years as a navvy and I had to sit at my books and learn to read and write! So you've a head start of me."

George was not to be comforted. "It's not just here – it's all the time – I never do things right – not for Mr Jellicoe – or for Ma. . . ."

There was a sudden silence. Robbie bent forward and knocked the ash from his pipe into the fire. "How about some tea before you go?" he said.

He poured water from the hissing kettle into the brown teapot. "Ye'll find cups on that shelf over there," he said and nodded in the direction.

George stood up and for the first time that evening he thought about something other than his troubles.

"Grandfather . . . ?"

"Aye?"

"I . . . just . . . wondered – why Ma made you up a can of tea when . . ." he broke off in confusion, feeling that he had been terribly rude, and his distress grew when Robbie burst out laughing.

George had never before seen his grandfather laugh, and he was amazed at the way his face changed. It seemed to light up from within. "I can see you've discovered my secret," Robbie chuckled. "Now how long have I been living with you and your mother?"

"I don't know . . . a few weeks I suppose."

"Aye . . . a few weeks . . . that's how long it was . . ." The smile vanished, blotted out by the pain of memory, and George fleetingly saw again that same expression on his grandfather's face that had been so terrible – so lonely.

"Anyway," Robbie said, and the expression was gone. "Anyway, every day I go to work your mother has filled a can of tea and made me up some food. And I haven't been able to tell her that I can make my own tea, fresh, or that Mrs Goodwin down at The Ship sends up a bit of stew or a slice of pie every day." He chuckled again. "I'm a very spoilt old man."

"Why don't you tell Ma?" George asked, confused.

Robbie finished pouring out the tea and handed George a cup. As he did so he stared straight at George, a steady, direct look and George suddenly understood. "It isn't that easy . . ." Robbie said gently, then went on more firmly, "and don't you be telling her either."

"Oh no! I couldn't!"

"No. Well," Robbie took a sip of tea, "now your brother is married and set up his own home, your mother will look to you for support."

"Me? Oh no!"

"Aye. She will."

George bit his lip. "Mother doesn't – doesn't like me," he said painfully. "Sometimes I think – she hates me."

There was a silence.

"You never knew your father did you?" Robbie asked thoughtfully.

"A bit. Not very well."

"He died fighting for his country against the Boers," Robbie said abruptly. "That made me proud – very proud." He stopped. "It broke your grandmother's heart though. My Deborah never really got over it."

A bell sounded, making George jump. Robbie went over to the train register and wrote something down, checking the time from the clock.

"This trouble you've had today. It will pass. Everything does. Sometimes too quickly." Robbie sighed and sat down. "Don't heed too much what Albert said to you – I'm sure he spoke in anger and didn't mean the half of it. He's a lot of worries of his own right now."

George stared into the fire.

"You must be getting home for your tea," said Robbie. He went on hesitantly. "If – if there's anything an old man like me can do to help – ye'll come and ask . . . ?"

George looked up and found Robbie smiling gently at him. How could he ever have been afraid of his grandfather? Why hadn't he realised that behind the old, sad face was a friend? "Ye're very like your father you know," Robbie said wistfully. "In a lot of ways."

He cleared his throat noisily, reached for his pipe and relit it with old hands that trembled very slightly.

"Here – look at George!" Ted called, hanging precariously off the engine's footplate as the train moved along the platform. When it stopped, Ted leapt off and raced over to him. "My – you're spruced up," Ted said admiringly. "I didn't recognise you."

George looked down self-consciously at his brand-new uniform. "It only came yesterday,' he said. "The sleeves are a bit long though . . ."

"Have to pay to talk to you soon," said Ted. "And I thought I'd impress you by being on the footplate!"

George grinned. "Driving or firing?" he asked.

"Only watching," Ted said ruefully. "Mind, I've done a bit of firing in the yard. Shunting engines round."

George began to unload beer barrels from the train with feverish haste. "I must get on," he said. "Mr Jellicoe's coming."

"I'll give you a hand," Ted said.

Mr Jellicoe was frowning when he reached them. "I think your driver is expecting you," he said pointedly to Ted.

"Yes sir!" Ted replied cheekily, winked at George and ran off.

Mr Jellicoe looked displeased. He turned to George. "Grant – I want you to run up to the Co-op," he said. "Tell Mr Wellerby that the flour he's been expecting has arrived from the docks and does he want to send his lad to collect it or can it wait until tomorrow when Alf Mason can take it round?"

"Yes, Mr Jellicoe."

George walked up the platform and, as he was passing the engine, Ted whistled and leaned over the side of the cab.

"Here! George!" he called in a loud whisper. George stopped. "Driver Wilson says if you have any trouble with Jelly, just ask how his missis is."

George squinted up at Ted. "His what?" he asked.

"His wife. Ask how his wife is."

"Why . . . ?"

But Ted just grinned and ducked back inside the cab.

George was puzzled for a moment. Perhaps his wife is ill, he thought, then dismissed Mr Jellicoe from his mind as he caught sight of his strange, uniformed reflection in a window. George was proud, very proud, of his uniform. It fitted him properly for a start – apart from the sleeves – and he no longer had to fear leaving a trail of burst buttons wherever he went. It also made him feel, for the first time, that he belonged to the station.

George had not had an easy working life since the sheep and pigs catastrophe. He had been the butt of many coarse jokes both from the station staff and from some of the passengers. Then his mother had made some pertinent comments about incompetence and stupidity, all of which were true, and all of which hurt.

Mr Jellicoe had never again alluded to the matter after that initial masterly telling-off, but he had been ten times harder to please and watched everything George did with an extra-critical eye.

But there had been one consolation for George. At the end of each day he could cross the track to the comfort of his grandfather's signalbox. They did not talk much. George would sit on a seat by the fire, hugging a cup of tea, watching his grandfather at work, recording and transmitting messages, pulling off signals, taking out tokens and disappearing from the box to exchange them with the drivers. He would watch him darn his socks, smoke his pipe and polish the brass bells. Everything grandfather did was at the same controlled, unhurried pace, and he took as much care in writing up his train register as he did in darning the smallest hole in one of his socks.

Grandfather's signalbox gave George a feeling of peace that he had never known before. The trains passed to and fro far below and the real world seemed light years away.

One evening, as he sat there, George said suddenly, "I wouldn't mind being a signalman."

"Aye?" said Robbie.

"It's so comfortable – and friendly here," George said. "No one tells you what to do."

Robbie smiled. "Ye're far and away out laddie," he said. "It's a lonely job at the best of times and it's an awful weight of responsibility." He stopped to answer a bell. "Think of it this way. A train driver relies on what the signals say as to whether it's safe to go on, slow down, or stop. He can't see very far ahead and he can't stop that quickly. So if the signalman makes a mistake and puts a signal at clear when the way ahead isn't safe – and there's an accident, and people get hurt – well then the signalman is responsible and not the driver."

Robbie pulled off the signals and took out a token. "I wouldna' like that on my conscience even if I was sitting snug in my box while it happened," he said, then went out with the token.

George sat thinking. He had imagined grandfather's job to be as comfortable and as remote as grandfather's signalbox, but he was wrong. He had thought that the signalman's job could be done in isolation from anyone else and that had appealed to him. He could not have been more wrong. It occurred to him, for the first time, that all his mistakes, everything he did, in fact everything *anyone* did, had an affect on other people in some way or another. It was not a comforting thought, and George shivered suddenly in the warm signalbox.

The next morning the staff inspection was cancelled without explanation and there was no sign of Mr Jellicoe. George fleetingly wondered if his wife really was ill.

But late that afternoon, Holmes called over to him. "Here Grant! Jelly wants you!"

George rapidly thought over the mistakes he had made that day and his heart beat uncomfortably. "D-does he? Why?" he asked.

"I don't know, do I?" was Holmes's unsympathetic reply.

George went to the office and tapped nervously at the door. The abrupt "Come!" from within did nothing to reassure him, and he went in fearfully, pulling off his cap as he did so. He closed the door behind him and looked at Mr Jellicoe.

Mr Jellicoe was sitting at his desk aimlessly riffling through some papers. His hat was off and his usually immaculate hair disarrayed. His stiff shirt collar had wilted, and there was a speck of dirt on his unbuttoned waistcoat. George was shocked. Mr Jellicoe's face was ashen and lined. He looked like some sad, ageing bloodhound.

"You wanted to see me Mr Jellicoe?" George asked.

Mr Jellicoe looked up and his eyes were blank. "What's

that?" he said, and even his voice sounded different, lost and vague, without its usual hard, precise edge. "Oh – yes, Grant."

He stared vacantly at George. The train pulled into the station and Mr Jellicoe started at the noise. He stood up and reached for his hat. "I'll just see the 5.10 gets off on time," he said. "Wait there."

He put on his hat and went out. George moved to the window and watched as Mr Jellicoe hurried down the platform, his coat flying, his hat askew. He chivvied the passengers impatiently, which was most unlike him, for however harsh Mr Jellicoe might be to his staff, he was always unfailingly courteous to his passengers. Now he appeared to be speaking sharply to the engine-driver, also unlike the correct, protocol-conscious Mr Jellicoe.

Eventually the train departed and George hastily moved away from the window. Mr Jellicoe burst in. "Those drivers!" he exploded in a taut, strained voice. "Think there's all the time in the world when they've got those silly girls to talk to . . . ! I've known the 5.10 arrive fifteen minutes late . . . *fifteen* minutes! Unforgiveable!"

He took off his hat and passed his hand across his eyes. "The coming of the railway brought time and order to this country, Grant, don't forget that – it brought railway time." He stopped and stared blankly at George.

"Yes Mr Jellicoe."

"You must study Grant, you must learn," Mr Jellicoe said, and his voice was quiet, empty of all expression, as if his mind and his thoughts were far, far away. "The correct time is carried by train from London. The guard on the first down train sets his watch by the station clock at Paddington and it is passed down the line to every succeeding station all over the country. Our own station clock is set each day by the time on the guard's watch arriving on the six o'clock miner's train from Kidderminster."

He stopped again and his eyes suddenly focused on George. "What are you wanting?" he asked vaguely.

"You wanted to see me Mr Jellicoe," said George.

"Did I?" Mr Jellicoe ran his hands through his hair, leaving it wilder than ever. "Oh yes. Yes." He looked at his desk and subsided into the chair. "So much to do . . ." he said in a distracted way. "Oh yes – I want you to repaint the platform edge line. We're expecting a station inspection and we mustn't . . ." He lost track of what he was saying. ". . . oh yes – you'll find the paint in the shed."

George waited for a moment, unsure whether he should stay or go. Mr Jellicoe suddenly pulled himself together. "Go on," he said in much his old manner. "What are you waiting for?"

George escaped from his office with relief and for a while he puzzled about Mr Jellicoe, but he soon became absorbed in his job. He liked painting and was careful to make a neat edge. When he finished, he stood back to admire his handiwork.

"That's a fine piece of work George," Robbie called over from the signalbox. "Come up and have some tea before you go. You can admire it properly from up here."

It was late by the time Grandfather and George had finished tea. George followed Robbie out of the signalbox and watched while he exchanged tokens with the driver of the heavily-laden coal train.

"You go off home laddie," said Robbie as he passed George on his way back to the box, but George remained to see the train depart. The gradient was steep south of Highley and the engine driver was having difficulty starting with the weight of thirty coal trucks to pull. As the engine had been standing the driver was forced to open the cylinder drain-cocks to release water trapped in them. Water and steam poured down onto the track at tremendous pressure throwing the ballast packed around the rails up on the platform.

The engine was quickly enveloped in clouds of steam. The driver released sand onto the rails to get a better grip, and finally, with a loud hiss, the train departed and George started to cross the track.

There was a howl of anguish from the platform and, as the smoke and steam cleared away, George could see Mr Jellicoe at the platform's edge, incoherent with rage, widly waving his fist at the departing train. "I – I'll get you for this . . . I'll put you on report . . . I'll have you fired . . . my beautiful platform . . . just you wait, Driver Castle . . . I'll fix you!"

Robbie poked his head out of the signalbox. "What's going on?" he asked. "What's amiss?"

"It's the coal train," George explained. "I think it blew ballast up on the platform – over the line I painted."

"Well it's no' the end of the world," Robbie said testily. "Albert does get carried away at times." He disappeared back inside and George turned to see Mr Jellicoe come out of the shed with a mop and bucket of water.

He wet the mop and began to wash down the platform. George watched for a moment or two. There was no one else around. Mr Jellicoe, the fearsome Mr Jellicoe, looked a sad, lonely figure as he worked away.

George crossed the track to the platform and Mr Jellicoe looked up, surprised. To George's dismay there were bright, unshed tears in Mr Jellicoe's eyes. "Grant! Did you see it? Throw up the dirt and ballast all over the platform? It's not allowed – strictly against the rules. And the station inspection due . . . all my paperwork waiting. But I'll get him. Oh yes indeed!"

He thrust the mop viciously into the bucket. George hesitated, then said, "If you like – I don't mind staying. I'll do that – if you like."

Mr Jellicoe stared at George, a blank, expressionless stare, then silently handed him the mop.

It was quite dark by the time George had finished and he

was very weary. He knocked on Mr Jellicoe's door and put his head round. "I've finished, Mr Jellicoe. I'll just put the things away."

Mr Jellicoe looked up from his paperwork. He, too, looked weary, and there were deep lines in his face George had never noticed before. "Right Grant," said Mr Jellicoe. "Er – thank you."

He paused for a moment. "Would you like to come round to the house when you're ready? I'll get you a bite to eat and some tea – if you're not in a hurry that is."

"Oh – thank you," George said, surprised. No one, as far as he knew, had ever been invited into Mr Jellicoe's house.

But as he followed Mr Jellicoe down the long corridor that led to the kitchen, George wished he had made some excuse not to come. The house seemed cold and cheerless and George felt awkward and embarrassed.

Mr Jellicoe led the way into the kitchen, but George stopped in the doorway, in utter amazement. The kitchen was in a dreadful mess. Heaps of clothes and papers filled the chairs, the remains of a half-finished meal stared depressingly from the table, and piles of dirty plates lay in the sink. The floor needed sweeping and the mantelpiece was thick with dust. There was no fire and the remains of ashes were spread out over the hearth. Mr Jellicoe's kitchen was so unlike the neat, the clean, the fastidious Mr Jellicoe that George felt he must be dreaming.

Mr Jellicoe was hurriedly sweeping plates and dishes off the table, talking disjointedly, obviously embarrassed. "I'm sorry – the mess – I didn't remember. Sit down, sit down. I won't be a minute. I don't know what food . . . ?"

He disappeared into a pantry and emerged with half a loaf of stale bread and some cheese. He put these down on the table in front of George.

"There now. It's not much – but you must be hungry. Growing lads always are."

He started to cut the bread with hands that trembled then abandoned the attempt and picked up the kettle. George stared at him in wonder.

"Help yourself. Help yourself."

George obediently cut himself a slice of bread, although he was not at all hungry, and Mr Jellicoe filled the kettle with water. "It's very difficult, all this – when you're not used to it. I've been so busy . . . I've had no time . . ." and he sat down suddenly in a defeated sort of way, the kettle still in his hand.

"Is – is Mrs Jellicoe – away then?" George asked diffidently, feeling he had to say something.

Mr Jellicoe looked at him strangely. "Mrs Jellicoe? Yes. I suppose she is. Yes. In a manner of speaking." He stood up and put the kettle down on the unlit range.

"Is – is she on holiday?" George asked. He was suddenly very scared. He did not want to know any more, he wanted to run away from these complicated adult things he did not understand.

"She's gone. She's never coming back. My Nancy."

There was a long silence. Mr Jellicoe began to pace round the room. "You won't tell anyone will you?" he asked. "No one must know."

"No . . . I . . ."

"She left me yesterday. Gone off with a tinker. Some common thief I'll be bound." He was still pacing round the room, hurt and bitter. "I don't know why. She had a nice home – every comfort – everything – I didn't grudge her a penny. All our own vegetables I grew – kept chickens . . . she wanted a new sideboard – I got one sent up from Worcester within a week – very best oak it was . . . everything . . ."

He stopped pacing and his face worked strangely. "The disgrace – I couldn't face it if anyone knew. People in my position must set an example in every way – in their private lives as well as in the Company's service."

"I . . . won't . . . tell . . ." said George, but Mr Jellicoe was not listening.

"I loved her. I still do." He seemed to crumple into a chair and put his head in his hands. "I don't know what I did wrong . . . I just don't know . . . that's the worst part . . . not knowing . . ."

George stood up. "I must go," he said. "Mother'll be . . ."

Mr Jellicoe looked up. "Of course," he said. "Thank you for staying. You're a good lad. You'll see yourself out . . .?"

George nodded.

"You steer clear of women, Grant," Mr Jellicoe called as George went to the door. "Don't get yourself entangled."

"Goodnight then . . ." George said, but Mr Jellicoe did not answer. He was staring blankly at the dirty plates on the table.

George closed the door gently behind him and took a deep, deep breath of station air. Poor Mr Jellicoe, he thought. Poor Mr Jellicoe!

9

The 3.10 departed in a fine flurry of steam and Highley Station was left with a few travel-weary passengers making for the exit, a quantity of miscellaneous goods to be sorted and the peace and quiet of a country station until the arrival of the 4.40 goods. It was the time George liked best, when the noise and the bustle died down and the station reverted to its usual sleepy afternoon quiet.

That afternoon was a particularly sleepy one with the station dozing in the early spring sunshine. The daffodils George had tended made a carpet of gold along the platform fence, and birds sang in the trees behind the signalbox. Even the distant sound of coal trucks being shunted blended into the peace of the afternoon.

George manoeuvred a heavily laden trolley deftly into a small space behind the shed and caught sight of the girl waiting on the platform. She was a small girl, about George's age, with thin features and brown hair. She looked as though she were waiting for someone.

George unloaded his trolley, then straightened up and glanced round. The girl was still there, now sitting forlornly on a large trunk. He dusted his hands against the seat of his trousers and went over. "Can I help you miss?" he asked.

The girl looked up. She had brown eyes and a pert, upturned nose. "What's that?" she said. She spoke with a strong accent George had never heard before.

"Carry your trunk?" he offered.

"Oh. I don't know. I thought I'd be met," she said, looking round.

"By whom?" asked George.

"Someone up at the big house. It said in this letter see . . ." She stood up, and she was quite short, barely reaching George's shoulder. She extracted a much-crumpled letter from her pocket. "I had to catch the train from Kidderminster at quarter to three, and I'd be met at Highley by someone from the big house. That's Mr William Crowhurst's isn't it?"

"Yes," said George.

"I can't read proper myself but it was read out to me till I learnt it." Her face fell. "I suppose I got it wrong – wouldn't be the first time neither. Is it far?"

"Only a mile or two," George said. "I'll give you a hand with the trunk if you like."

"Are you allowed to?"

"Just let me ask permission, miss," George said, and raced off to find Mr Holmes. Permission given, he returned to the girl, picked up the heavy trunk, staggered under its weight and preceded her off the station.

The road was steep and the girl walked briskly. George sweated under the weight of the trunk and tried to keep up.

"He's a mill owner isn't he?" she said, turning back to wait for him.

"Who?" George panted.

"Mr Crowhurst up at the big house."

"No. He owns the mines round here."

"I didn't know there was any mines," she said. "Mind you, I've never been this way before."

George put the trunk down and mopped his brow. "Where are you from?" he asked curiously.

"Birmingham," she replied. "Well, near enough. But me mother's Irish which is why I've got a bit of an accent."

George picked up the trunk, but the girl took one handle and they made better progress.

"What will you be doing here?" George asked, then wondered whether he ought to ask so many questions. The girl did not seem to mind, though, in fact she seemed eager to talk.

"I've got a position," she said proudly. "It's me first one too. Under kitchen-maid. I'm to be paid £20 a year, although mother says I'll probably have to pay it all back for things I break."

"Do you break things?" George asked in surprise.

"Awful clumsy I am," she confessed.

"So am I," he confided, delighted to find someone afflicted like himself.

They did not speak again until they reached the big house. George glanced at the girl and he was surprised to see that she looked nervous. She had seemed such a self-possessed person.

"Where do I go, do you think?" she asked George.

He led the way to the back door, having been there before delivering messages. "Here," he said. "I'll pull the bell for you."

He put down the trunk and pulled loudly on the bell. "Someone'll help you in with your trunk," he said, and hesitated, feeling awkward. "I'd better be off."

The girl smiled at him. "You're very kind."

George turned pink with pleasure. "Well – all the best with the job."

"Thank you."

"Perhaps . . .?"

"What?"

"You'll come down to the station sometime," George finished, acutely embarrassed.

She smiled again. "If I can."

The door opened and a superior manservant looked down at them. The girl drew in a quick, scared breath and turned to George. "Well, 'bye then," she said.

"'Bye."

George walked off, pleased, confused and uncomfortable all at once. He felt a warm sympathy for her, not only because she was starting work, but also for admitting to being "awful clumsy" as well. He thought about her over the next few days and wondered how she was and if he would ever see her again.

It was just one week later when he caught sight of her. He was hurrying to work and saw her coming over the hill, a basket on her arm. As soon as she saw him, she waved and ran to meet him.

"Hello," she said.

"Hello," George replied shyly.

"Aren't you the person who helped me with me trunk?"

"That's right."

She took his arm and walked on with him. "You know, they'd forgotten all about me coming like," she confided.

"Oh," said George, nervous at having her small hand tucked through his arm.

"Sure, it doesn't matter though," she said. "It's a bit like that."

"What is?"

"Them up there," she said, jerking her head in the direction of the big house. "They're not a bit friendly-like, if you know what I mean."

George did know. "Aren't they?" he said sympathetically.

"Oh, I don't mind them," she said defiantly. "Apart from feeling a bit lonely at times."

"Do you have to work hard?" he asked.

"Yes. Hard enough." She glanced at George. "But I got a half-day off this Sunday."

George gulped and looked at the ground.

"Is the country nice round here?" she asked.

"Yes. I suppose so," said George, surprised. He had never thought about it before. "There's . . . woods . . . and fields . . . and the river."

She gave a cry of delight. "Well, fancy that now! I always liked a bit of water, so I did."

"You can get a rowing boat out further down – at Arley," George said, encouraged.

"Can you now? It sounds awful nice." she sighed. "A pity though, I can't row."

George knew what he wanted to say, but it took him a full thirty seconds of stammering and stuttering before he could say it. "Well . . . I . . . would you . . . that is . . . I'll take you . . . only . . . if you'd like . . ." he trailed off lamely.

"That's a nice idea," said the girl, smiling at him. She thought for a moment. "We could go this Sunday. On my half-day off."

George spent the rest of that week in an agony of worry. He thought over and over their conversation. Had he been too forward in his suggestion? He had no experience as to what one said or what one did when asking a young lady out and he was sure that somehow he had made a mess of it. But she did agree to go with me he thought, which made him feel a little better.

Then further worries assailed him. A boat on the river seemed such an easy thing, but was actually very difficult, not least because George was not a particularly good oarsman. Then he was not very sure either whether boats could be hired at that time of year, when the river was often in full flood. Terrible visions rose in his mind of a swollen River Severn intent on hurtling him and the girl downstream to a very nasty end, and he went down to the river to examine it. The fact that it looked as flat and calm as a mill-pond did little to reassure him.

Another worry occurred to him. He had not arranged a time to meet and he flinched from the idea of marching up to the house to ask for her. His heart fell with a thud. How could he go and ask for her – he did not even know her name! He could hardly demand the new under kitchen-maid from that superior manservant.

After a sleepless night he decided that he would just have to hang round the grounds in the hope that she would emerge. They'll probably set their dogs on me as a trespasser, he thought gloomily and then worried about what he would say to her during that long afternoon, always supposing she had not changed her mind about going out with him after all.

That's probably what will happen he thought as he surveyed his round face in the mirror, she won't turn up. She can't want to go out with *me!*

But George need not have worried, for when he finally arrived at the big house with scrubbed face, slicked-down hair and a tumult of conflicting feelings, she was there waiting for him.

Her name was Annie and George thought she was quite wonderful. She sat in the boat – which George had managed to hire at an exorbitant price – trailing one hand in the water, a dainty parasol protecting her complexion from the delicate spring sunshine.

George sat at the other end of the boat, red-faced and sweating as he rowed hard against the spring current.

Annie sighed. "This is really nice," she said. "I do like the country. It's so – peaceful. But then I like a bit of fun now and again, don't you? Bit of excitement – if you know what I mean."

George did not know what she meant, but as he had no breath left with which to speak anyway, he just grunted, and any worries about what they would talk about fled before her constant chatter.

"A drink or two and a dance with some friends," she went on with hardly a pause. "Trouble is they're all so stiff up at the house. They can't let themselves go. Cook gave me a right tellin' off the other day because she found James – he's one of the footmen – an' me havin' a bit of a jig in the kitchen. Mean old cow!"

George was shocked, but whether it was at the idea of Annie and James having a jig, or at Annie's choice of language, or because Cook had told Annie off, he was not sure. He felt confused, and concentrated on rowing.

"I don't think I'll stay there too long," Annie was saying. "It doesn't really suit me. Perhaps I'll get a position in London. Plenty of life there."

George rested his oars for a moment. "I've never been to London," he said.

"Honest now?"

"I've been to Worcester though. To Divisional Head-quarters. For a medical."

Annie looked at him in a wondering way. "Don't you find it dull here at all?" she asked.

George thought hard. "No," he said.

"Oh well, it takes all sorts as mum says." She settled herself more comfortably in the boat and smiled at George. "This is real nice," she said. George smiled back and, with a sigh, resumed rowing.

It was a wonderful afternoon. The sun shone and the birds sang and Annie smiled, talked and looked pretty. George let the boat drift into the bank and helped Annie out. She sat on his coat under a willow tree, shaded by the fresh green of the young leaves and George tied up the boat and sat beside her on the muddy ground. He kept looking at her. She was so dainty and fragile, he thought, just like – just like a piece of his mother's best china teaset.

Annie sent George off to pick early catkins and George muddied his trousers and covered himself with yellow pollen in his efforts to pick the longest and the prettiest. But he did not mind. No – for once he never even thought of what his mother would say. It was a wonderful, wonderful afternoon!

IO

The unusual sight of Alfred Holmes perfunctorily wielding a duster round the waiting room early Monday morning startled some of the passengers and their wait was not a comfortable one, for the entire station staff seemed intent on turning the place upside down.

A gentleman trying to purchase a ticket was told to "wait a moment, please sir" while Reginald Davies finished balancing the books, then entered the totals into his ledger in his immaculate copperplate handwriting. It was more than a minute the gentleman had to wait, but when he tried to complain to the Stationmaster he was brushed aside, for on this one day of the year Mr Jellicoe was not attentive to the wishes of his passengers. He was far too busy masterminding the whole operation of making the station ready for its annual inspection.

Holmes, Harvey and George had arrived a full hour early and were scurrying through their chores at breakneck speed, and Mr Wrighton was fully engaged in the sidings, trying to shunt the coal wagons into some semblance of neatness.

Even Robbie was caught up in the excitement. He gave his signalbox a special clean and selected a fresh cloth to use when pulling off the signals.

The early train arrived, but the staff were far too busy to attend to the wants of the passengers and the gentleman who had had difficulty buying his ticket spent a pleasant journey composing an irate letter to send to the District Headquarters about the gross inefficiency of Highley Station.

Ted jumped off the footplate in great excitement and looked round for George. "George! Hey George! Have you heard?"

"What?"

"Your station inspection. It's gone all round the yard that some top nob from Paddington is coming to it."

"Why?" George asked.

"I don't know, do I?" said Ted.

"What are you doing here?"

Ted swelled up with pride. "Been sent to act as fireman for the colliery engine," he said. "Their fireman's off sick and Mr Jellicoe wanted some coal trucks shunted out of the way."

"Grant! Grant – come here!" Mr Jellicoe came out of his office and looked round for George.

"I'd better go," Ted said. "Fun isn't it?"

Mr Jellicoe bore down on them and sent Ted off with a withering glance. "Grant – get all the staff together. I want everyone here – immediately. It appears we are to have an Important Visitor at our inspection."

When the train carrying the inspection party arrived from the south, Highley Station was fully prepared. The staff were standing rigidly to attention: hats were on straight; shoes and buttons gleamed; hair was neatly brushed. Even Fry's tie was no longer crooked. "I'm not having you letting me down, Fry," Mr Jellicoe had said as he personally wrenched the tie into position.

The train stopped, the door opened and Mr Colebatch, the District Superintendent, came out followed by Inspector Hunt from Worcester, the travelling audit clerk, and lastly the Important Visitor – Mr Allen, the Superintendent of the Line. Introductions were performed and the inspection started.

A hush fell over the station for the next hour while the inspection continued. The books were thoroughly examined by the audit clerk, while the rest of the party inspected the staff, then wandered round the station making sure there were no weeds on the platform, no dust in the waiting room, and nothing untoward anywhere.

Of course no fault could be found with Mr Jellicoe's station, and the inspection drew to an end. Bit of an anti-climax thought George, impassively waiting while the party assembled on the platform. He was not sure exactly what he had expected but he felt a bit let down. Then Mr Jellicoe beckoned him. "Ask Mr Grant to step down here for a moment Grant," he said.

George was momentarily puzzled. "Mr . . .?" he said. It seemed odd to hear Grandfather being called Mr Grant. "Oh yes, Mr Jellicoe," he said and went off to the signalbox.

Mr Allen stared after George. "His son?" he asked.

"His grandson, sir," Mr Jellicoe replied.

"Jolly good," said Mr Allen.

"The family traditions of this Company undoubtedly contribute to its success," Mr Colebatch put in. "It ensures stability among its staff."

"Quite," replied Mr Allen dryly.

George and Robbie approached the group. Robbie was looking puzzled and carried a token in his hand.

"Mr Grant, Mr Colebatch," Mr Jellicoe said, and Mr Colebatch shook hands heartily with Robbie.

"Mr Grant, I have a very pleasant duty to perform today," he said. "For the past forty years you have been a faithful and conscientious servant of the Great Western Railway Company. You have carried out your duties in a diligent and responsible manner which has brought credit to the Company we all serve. I therefore have the greatest pleasure in presenting you with this engraved time piece and gold albert on behalf of the Company. Mr Allen, if you would be . . .?"

He handed the watch and chain to Mr Allen who presented them to Robbie and shook his hand. Robbie looked dazed, and George, together with the rest of the staff and the few passengers who had been craning their necks to see what was happening, cheered and cheered.

They were still cheering that night in the less constrained atmosphere of the pub. All the station staff and Ted were there, crowded round Robbie, examining the watch and chain.

"Fair bowled over, I havena' got over it," Robbie said, still slightly dazed. He chuckled. "I thought I was to be getting the sack when George came to get me."

Everyone laughed.

"No man better deserves it," said Mr Jellicoe firmly.

Ted and George eased away from the crowd and sat down.

"Old Jelly's actually smiling," Ted said. "How's he been treating you?"

"Oh – not so bad," said George.

"Did you need Driver Wilson's advice by the way?" Ted asked. "What was it about his wife? Did you find out?"

George thought back to that night in Mr Jellicoe's kitchen, with his sad, defeated figure slumped among all the dirty pots and pans. "Whatever your Driver Wilson meant, he got it wrong," he said.

Ted looked at him, surprised. "You're very sure."

"I am," said George firmly. "Mr Jellicoe's all right. When you get to know him."

"If you say so," said Ted wryly into his beer glass.

"I do."

George did not know the outcome of Mrs Jellicoe's disappearance. Mr Jellicoe had never spoken of it of course and George could not ask. The day after he had broken down, Mr Jellicoe had seemed his old self and nothing had changed.

Or has it, George thought suddenly. He looked over to where Mr Jellicoe was standing, flushed and beaming. Was Mr Jellicoe a bit more human, a bit more approachable? Or was it that George was no longer afraid of him, had lost his fear that night in Mr Jellicoe's kitchen?

George finished his drink thoughtfully and he and Ted went out. They started to argue, as they often did. "Railways are about *engines*," Ted insisted. "They're the only things that're important."

"Aren't you forgetting the passengers?" George said. "Aren't they what it's about? Providing a service to get them where they want to go?"

"Well, there you are. What takes them there? Engines!" Ted said triumphantly. "You forget that, stuck away in your little station. That's the trouble with old Jelly – well, part of it. He thinks trains are a nuisance, messing up his nice platforms."

"Platform. There's only one at Highley," George grinned. "You should get to know the line better, Ted. And it's not like that," he went on earnestly. "The station's right at the centre of it all. Everything comes and goes from here. Not just people – newspapers, goods, post . . . everything. It's like being right at the heart of things. That's the bit I like."

"What would the stations be without trains?" said Ted. "Nothing."

"I'd like to run my own station one day," George said thoughtfully. "Then it belongs to you in a funny sort of way – you don't have to move or anything – it all comes to you."

"You're an old stick-in-the-mud," Ted jeered. "Don't you want change, excitement, bit of adventure?"

"Not really," George said honestly. "I'll leave that to people like you."

They walked on in companionable silence for a while.

"You working Sunday?" Ted asked abruptly.

"No."

"Like to go fishing?"

George paused for a moment. "I'm sorry. I can't."

"Your mum, is it?" Ted asked in quick sympathy.

"N–no."

Something in George's voice made Ted stare at him, a knowing grin spreading on his face.

"I'm going out. It's all fixed up," George said hastily.

Ted stopped. "It's never – George, you sly old thing – I didn't know you were courting!"

George blushed bright red.

If this was courting, it was a bit uncomfortable, George thought as he scrambled up the bank after Annie. She had suggested a stroll in the country and George had been following her for the last hour as she strode through woods and across fields with tireless energy, talking all the time.

When she finally sat down for a rest, George was relieved. She smiled at him. "Do you think I'm pretty?" she asked.

"Oh yes . . ." George said fervently.

"I wanted to go on the stage . . . you know – in the Music Halls – but mum said I ought to get a trade."

They sat in silence for a minute. "Do you ever want to do anything else?" she asked.

George thought for a moment. "Not really," he said at last. "I never really thought about it. It's in the family you see. To work for the railway."

"And do you like it?"

"It's all right. Parts of it I do – parts I don't. Like anything else."

"If my mum was here she'd want to know if it had prospects, if you know what I mean. Very hot on them, my mum is."

George played with a blade of grass. "Well, in time – if I work hard – I could end up Stationmaster," he said humbly.

"At one of them big stations like Paddington?" she said, prepared to be impressed.

George could not deceive her. "Well – no. Somewhere round here."

She smiled at him, but it was a different smile, a slightly amused, superior, smile. "Bit of a stick-in-the-mud, aren't you George," she said lightly.

He knew he was. Ted had told him so, and now Annie. He stared at his blade of grass. "Yes – I suppose I am," he replied honestly. "I wouldn't be good enough for any of the big stations anyway."

Annie stood up suddenly. "Will you take me back please? I've got to be in by six."

Silently they retraced their steps over the fields to the big house. The magic had gone from the afternoon, if it had ever been there to start with.

Annie stopped as the house came into view. "You'd best leave me here," she said.

"Why?" George asked.

"Well, you know what they're like up there – gossip," she said.

George did not know, but nodded wisely. "Oh, of course."

"Thank you for this afternoon," she said.

"Did you like it?" he asked eagerly.

She smiled, a friendly smile. "Oh yes, surely."

"So did I."

He could not think of anything else to say and they stood staring at each other.

"Well – goodnight," Annie said at last.

George put out his hand to shake hers. Annie ignored it.

"Aren't you going to kiss me?" she said, amused.

George took a tremulous breath. "Can I?" he asked.

"Yes. If you like."

He took off his cap, took a deep breath and pecked at her warm cheek. Then he jumped back as if he expected her to bite. Annie laughed and flicked his cheek with her finger.

"Sure – you're very young and very sweet so you are," she said and ran off.

George stared after her until she had disappeared into the house. She must have liked the afternoon, after all, he thought, she must have liked me. He felt overjoyed. In his mind he was already re-living every second of that beautiful afternoon as he turned and walked down the hill with squared shoulders and big, manly strides.

II

Mr Holmes entered the porters' room quietly, looked round, tiptoed over to the corner where George was sitting engrossed in a book, bent down and bellowed in his ear: "Grant!"

George jumped up, startled. "Sorry Mr Holmes."

"What's this you've got?" Holmes asked, picking up the book George had dropped. "*Great Western Railway. Additions to certain of the Rules in the general appendix to the Rule Book*," he read. "There's an industrious lad," he said with heavy sarcasm, throwing the book back at George. "Listen Grant, I've got to go off for an hour or two. See a man about a dog."

"A man . . .?"

"Private business, Grant, private business," said Holmes, tapping the side of his nose significantly. "No one should want me – it's Jelly's day off after all – but if anyone does – you'll make some excuse, right?"

"What sort of . . .?" George asked.

"Thick as two planks, you are sometimes," said Holmes,

exasperated. "Just hold the fort, will you? I won't be long."

He went out and George returned to his seat and his book. It was a sunny, peaceful afternoon. A whole hour contentedly spread out before him: an hour without any job to be done; an hour without anyone shouting for him; an hour before the next train was due; an hour he could spend with the sun streaming in through the window, warming his face while he wrestled with the *Additions to certain of the Rules* . . . He yawned loudly and the book started to slip from his grasp. Hurried footsteps sounded along the platform and a small, dapper man in a neat dark suit entered the porters' room. He looked round. "You – boy!"

George dropped his book once more, jumped up and fumbled for his hat. "Yes sir?"

"I want the Stationmaster – urgently." The man spoke in a clipped, precise way.

"The Stationmaster is off today, sir," said George.

"Well, who's in charge then?"

George looked round vaguely then straightened himself. "Anything I can do, sir?"

"I want a special train – a private one, in one hour's time, to convey an important personage to Shrewsbury."

"It's rather difficult at this short notice, sir," George said earnestly. "It would upset all the schedules. A booking for a special has to go through the correct channels . . ."

The man interrupted. "There has been a motor car breakdown. It is imperative that a special is provided in one hour."

George backed away nervously. "Perhaps if you'd care to speak to . . ."

"The train is required for His Majesty the King."

There was a stunned silence.

"The . . .?"

"Yes," said the dapper man. "I must return to him immediately. Send word to The Grafton Arms when the train is ready to depart. But I must impress upon you that His

Majesty has an urgent appointment in Shrewsbury at half-past three."

He walked off, leaving an open-mouthed George staring after him.

It took George a good few seconds to take in what the dapper man had said, and another few seconds to convince himself that he was quite awake and did not dream it. Then he raced out of the porters' room. Mr Jellicoe. He must find Mr Jellicoe.

He tried Mr Jellicoe's house, but no one answered the crescendo of hammering on the door. Then George raced to Mr Jellicoe's private garden, burst in and looked round, but there was no one there.

"Must think," thought George. "Where's he gone, where, where . . .?" He set off for the river, heart pounding, breath coming in short gasps, the butterflies in his stomach fluttering wildly. As he ran, the thought went through his head that it was a bit unfair of Mr Holmes to have left him with this crisis, not that Mr Holmes could have known that the King would break down in Highley and demand a special train! "The King," George thought, panic-stricken. "*The King!*. . . only got an hour . . . *must* find Mr Jellicoe . . . *must!*"

He found Mr Jellicoe at last. Mr Jellicoe was peacefully fishing on the riverbank, rod firmly wedged into the ground, head nodding on his chest.

"Mr Jellicoe! Mr Jellicoe!" George called as he pounded up to him. Mr Jellicoe gave a snort, a start, and raised his head.

"Wh–as that? Wh . . .?"

"Oh Mr Jellicoe – thank goodness you're here!" George stopped, fighting to get his breath back.

"What's that . . . Grant? What's . . .?"

"Mr Jellicoe – the King's coming. In an hour. *Please* Mr Jellicoe."

"What's all this Grant?" said Mr Jellicoe crossly. "What's going on? I thought I left strict instructions . . ."

"The King's coming. In an hour. He wants a train."

"Where's Holmes? Can't he deal with . . . the *who* . . .?"

"The King," said George. Words tumbled out, disjointedly. "He's broken down and waiting at The Grafton Arms and wants a train in an hour."

Mr Jellicoe blinked. "You must learn Grant, to pass on messages briefly and succinctly," he said. "Start at the beginning."

"There's no time, Mr Jellicoe," said George desperately. "A gentleman came and said that the King's motor car has broken down and that he's waiting at The Grafton Arms and to let him know when we have a special ready to take the King to Shrewsbury – but it has to be within an hour because the King has to be in Shrewsbury at half-past three." George stopped, breathless.

Mr Jellicoe slowly let the information sink in. "It sounds a tarradiddle to me," he said at last. "How did you know this man was who he said he was?"

George bit his lip. "I didn't . . . don't . . ." he said. The thought had never occurred to him.

"How did you know that he wasn't fabricating a tale in order to disrupt the workings of the Company?" Mr Jellicoe persisted.

"Well . . . why should he?" said George.

Mr Jellicoe pulled his rod out of the ground. "What evidence did he produce?" he asked.

George felt hot all over. "None," he said, then continued honestly, "but I didn't ask him for any."

"Get me Holmes and Davies," said Mr Jellicoe, getting up from his seat. "I must consider this."

"It's Mr Davies' day off and Mr Holmes . . ." George trailed off unhappily.

"I'll come myself and see him," said Mr Jellicoe and he started packing his things.

"He – he went off too," said George in a small voice.

Mr Jellicoe stared at George. "He did *what*?" he said aghast.

"Only for a short while," said George miserably. "He said – to – see a man about a dog."

There was a very nasty silence. "Mr Holmes has no business to have any other business other than the Company's during the Company's time," said Mr Jellicoe at last. "Now let me see . . ."

"I – I could go to The Grafton Arms and see if the man is there – and the King?" offered George.

"Yes – no! If the message is accurate then I shall need you here." Mr Jellicoe thought for a moment then looked hard at George and spoke in a serious voice. "Now Grant, think carefully. You seriously believe that the gentleman was telling you the truth?"

George thought hard. "Yes," he said.

"And you are absolutely sure that you have conveyed the message to me accurately?"

George thought again. The awful responsibility of it all frightened him. "Yes," he said again.

"Very well. Very well," said Mr Jellicoe. "I believe you. But I just hope for your sake that you are right."

He walked off and George picked up Mr Jellicoe's rod and stool. A small, icy fear, like a cold knot was forming in the pit of his stomach. He swallowed hard and followed Mr Jellicoe back to the station.

Once back at the station, Mr Jellicoe assumed full control. His first action was to go to the waiting room and peer in through the hatch to the ticket office.

Jonas Fry was sitting the other side, in the ticket office. He was comfortably esconsed, hat off, feet up on the counter, and he was chuckling over some story in the penny dreadful magazine he was reading.

"*Fry!*"

Fry leaped to his feet.

"I'll not reprimand you now for your slovenly appearance, but I shall later," said Mr Jellicoe grimly. "Ring through to Kidderminster – get Mr Dobson on the line and I will speak to him. Do it instantly! We have a crisis on our hands."

Mr Jellicoe turned to George. "Grant – it goes without saying that the station must look immaculate in one hour's time. See to it."

George started to go.

"But first inform your grandfather!" Mr Jellicoe called after him.

"Mr Dobson on the line, Mr Jellicoe," said Fry, and handed over the receiver.

Inside his grandfather's signalbox, George was finding difficulty in persuading Robbie to believe his story. "The King did you say? Edward VII?"

"Yes," said George.

"Here – at Highley station?" Robbie asked incredulously.

George nodded.

"Are ye *sure*, laddie?"

George nodded again, less certainly.

"Because if you're not – and a special train is being laid on – and the whole service suspended . . ." Robbie paused.

"What?" asked George in a small voice.

Robbie sighed. "Well, at least, I think you'll be looking for a new job."

"Oh," said George.

"Albert too, I would think."

There was a moment's silence.

"I *was* sure, until everyone started saying that," said George unhappily. "Now I *think* I'm sure. But then I do get things mixed up . . ."

12

Mr Jellicoe, at any rate, seemed to have no doubts about George's story. He was revelling in the situation.

"Grant!" he called, and George came running from the signalbox. "Grant! They're sending the tank engine with the District Superintendent's saloon. It's being cleaned on the way down. Wrighton's doing the waiting room, so you start on the platform."

George ran off to find a broom and Mr Jellicoe looked anxiously up and down the platform. "Thank goodness the platform edge has been done," he said as he went into his office.

The next half hour passed in intense activity. George had no time to reflect about the dapper gentleman as he swept the station from top to bottom then dusted and polished everything that could be dusted and polished. Mr Mason assisted him, but his assistance was of the most cursory kind.

"Look Grant," said Mr Mason. "If the King *does* come, he's going to be in too much of a hurry to notice whether the weighing machine has been cleaned. I really wouldn't bother."

But George did bother. He gave the machine a quick dust after Mr Mason had gone, then set about moving a laden wheelbarrow out of sight behind the shed.

Across the track, Robbie had put any doubts to one side and was assiduously cleaning his signalbox, even to the extent of leaning out precariously in order to polish the outside of the windows.

Mr Jellicoe spent some considerable time on the telephone then changed into his uniform. He went to the mirror hanging in his office, put on his hat with a solemn air and stared impassively at the face in front of him. He thought fleetingly that it was a pity he had not had time to have his whiskers trimmed for the occasion, then, with the utmost gravity, he practised for the great moment.

"Your *Majesty* – your *train*," he said. He tried again, shifting the emphasis: "*Your* Majesty – *your* train." He frowned at his reflection. "Your Majesty – here is your train." That might do, he thought, that might just do. He smiled suddenly as a pleasing thought crossed his mind. At last Highley Station, with Stationmaster Albert Arthur Jellicoe, would get a mention in the Great Western Railway Magazine.

George had just finished on the platform when Holmes strolled up with a casual, well-satisfied-with-the-world expression on his face. "Everything all right Grant?" he inquired breezily.

Mr Jellicoe's voice sounded blightingly in his ear. "Holmes. I shall deal with you later."

It was a very nasty shock for Holmes, and for a second he lost his customary assurance, "What's *he* doing here?" he mouthed to George.

"Carpet, Grant," Mr Jellicoe said decisively. "What we need is red carpet."

"Yes Mr Jellicoe," said George.

"Unfortunately there isn't any. And there's no time to get some up from Headquarters." Mr Jellicoe stopped and thought. "I know. Go to my house. Go up in the loft . . . there might be something there." He rounded on Holmes. "Go on – help him!"

The loft was dark and dirty. It was full of interesting-shaped boxes, stacked and labelled with Mr Jellicoe's customary neatness. George lifted his lamp and peered round. Behind him, Holmes kept up a steady stream of grumbling.

"I didn't know the King was going to come, did I?" he said in an injured voice. "I mean it's just not fair, is it?"

George spotted some rolled-up carpet and tried to open it out sufficiently in order to see what colour it was. "D'you think that will do?" he wondered, holding up a piece for Holmes to see.

"This chap I know," Holmes went on, not paying the slightest attention to George, "does a bit of poaching now and then – well he offered me a couple of hares and a brace of pheasant for the price of a drink . . . well, I couldn't turn that down could I?"

"It's better than nothing I suppose," George said doubtfully, after deep and lengthy contemplation of the piece of carpet. He straightened up and flashed his lamp round. "You take this down and I'll just see if there's anything else," he said, and Holmes disappeared down the rickety steps, clutching the carpet and still grumbling.

Out in the daylight, the carpet proved to be worn and threadbare, with the original pattern of crimson and orange flowers against a green background fortunately faded with time. Clouds of dust rose up as it was unrolled from the waiting room door to the platform edge. When it was down, Mr Jellicoe, Fry and Holmes surveyed it in silence.

"It's better than nothing," Mr Jellicoe said eventually.

George appeared just then, and took Mr Jellicoe's mind off

the carpet, for he was carrying bundles of faded red, white and blue bunting.

"I found this as well, Mr Jellicoe," George said.

"Well, bless my soul," said Mr Jellicoe, examining the limp flags which were criss-crossed with the dust of years. "I'd forgotten we had this. It was issued for the Queen's Jubilee. When was that . . . eight, nine years ago?"

"Shall I put it up?" George asked.

"Why not, Grant. Why not?" said Mr Jellicoe. He left the bunting with George and looked up the line. "Now where's that train?" he said, anxiously taking out his watch.

The special train was crossing Victoria Bridge, gleaming in the sunshine from the hurried clean it had received. Inside the District Superintendent's saloon Ted Jarvis was on his hands and knees brushing the thick carpet, while a fellow cleaner polished the mahogany writing desk with care.

"Makes a bit of a change from cleaning out the firebox," Ted commented as the train gathered speed after the bridge. It passed non-stop through Arley Station whistling shrilly, and the signalman picked up his telephone.

At Highley George was putting the finishing touches to the bunting. He had nailed it along the canopy and over the doors of the waiting room. The tired, dusty flags hung limply, and the old, threadbare carpet stretched across the platform as if surprised at being taken out of retirement.

George half-closed his eyes. That was better, he thought. If you did not look too closely, the overall impression *was* gay – it was certainly different.

"At least it shows we've tried," he said to Fry.

Robbie emerged from his signalbox. "George!" he called. "Tell Albert. The train's just passed through Arley."

"Train's coming Mr Jellicoe," said George, putting his head round the office door. Mr Jellicoe put on his hat with care and came out on to the platform. He turned solemnly to George.

"I want you to go to The Grafton Arms, Grant, and convey the message to His Majesty that the Great Western Railway Company has, at his express command, a train awaiting his pleasure at Highley Station to convey him to Shrewsbury."

Holmes, who was standing beside George, puffed out his chest and took a step forward. "Mr Jellicoe. As Head Porter I feel *I* should be the one to. . . ."

"You will count yourself fortunate Holmes, if you are still in the Company's employ at the end of the day," said Mr Jellicoe crisply. "Off you go Grant. And remember if you are fortunate enough to be addressed by His Majesty, that you represent the Great Western Railway."

George nodded, unable to speak, and went off. He left the station and hurried up the lane with a hunted look on his usually placid face and a cold fear in the pit of his stomach. His heart thudded uncomfortably and his lips mouthed, over and over again, "Please let it be the King . . . oh, please let it be the King . . ."

He hurried to the village, up the main street, past rows of shops, past people, not noticing anything or anybody. Then his arm was caught.

"George! Well isn't this nice now?"

He turned to find Annie smiling at him. "I can't stop Annie," he said.

"What's your rush?"

"Company business."

"Oh now . . ." Annie slipped her hand through his arm. "I was hoping to see you . . ."

"I must go," said George, desperately tearing himself free. "I've got to see the King."

"The what?"

"Tell you later," said George, and ran off in the direction of The Grafton Arms.

The special train steamed gently into Highley Station and

an excited Ted Jarvis poked his head out of the saloon. "Nearly fit for a King, Mr Jellicoe," he called cheerfully. "When's he arriving?"

"Soon. Soon." Mr Jellicoe was steadily growing more and more nervous. He paced the platform up and down, up and down, twitching things into place and out of place, and looked at his watch every other second.

"Hello Mr Holmes," said Ted, as Holmes strolled up. "Right old hornet's nest been stirred up at Kidder. Well, I've done my best, but it's not really what the King's been used to, I'll bet."

"Let's hope it's all worth it, shall we?" said Holmes sourly.

"Why?" asked Ted, astonished.

"Your friend young Grant took the message. From some strange man who just turned up on the platform. Let's hope there really is a King at the end of all this fuss. I doubt it though."

13

The Grafton Arms was a small hotel that had originated as a posting house. The coming of the railway had taken most of its overnight trade away and now the hotel survived mainly on local patronage, and the occasional letting to people on business connected with the mines.

When George arrived, the small courtyard was empty. George had half-imagined having to fight through crowds of cheering subjects and the sleepy normality of the hotel did nothing to reassure him that the dapper gentleman's story was true and that the King of England was indeed inside The Grafton Arms.

George was now quite sick with nerves, half brought on by the growing conviction that he had somehow got it all wrong again and there was no King, and half brought on by the slightly more terrifying prospect that he, George Grant, might be about to meet King Edward VII.

Surely there were special ways of behaving when talking

to a King, George thought, and vague ideas flitted through his mind about walking backwards and not speaking until spoken to.

He looked up at the black-and-white exterior and the blank windows. "Must get it over with," he thought, so he straightened his cap, brushed down his jacket, took a deep breath and, with legs that felt wobbly and unsafe, walked inside.

An enormously fat, elderly man, dressed in a dark suit, appeared from some back recess and walked up to George. The man, whom George knew to be the manager of the hotel, looked like a walking jelly, with great rolls of fat trembling whenever he moved.

"Yes?" said the manager, and the rolls quivered.

"I've come – from the station," stammered George. "To – to give a message to the – the King."

For an agonising moment the manager did not react at all. He just stared at George, small beady eyes poking out of his face, blank and expressionless. *I've got it all wrong*, George thought desperately, *oh no!*

"You'd better come this way then," the manager said finally, and led the way towards a flight of stairs.

George closed his eyes in a moment's sheer relief until the second wave of panic came over him. With unsteady legs he followed the broad, swaying back ahead of him.

"Thank goodness you've come," the manager said. "It's not that we don't like having His Majesty here – not that we're not deeply honoured – but it's a big responsibility you know and . . . well, here we are."

He stopped outside a door, knocked, and the door was immediately opened by a tall, thin man.

"The lad from the station, sir," said the manager, and pushed George forwards into the room.

The room was long and thin. George gained an impression of a once grand room now sad and dingy, its wallpaper turning brown with age and its carpet faded to an indistinguishable grey.

There was a group of men at the far end of the room and one of them moved forwards. George was inexpressibly relieved to see that it was his own dapper gentleman. "Well?"

"The – the train is waiting for His Majesty sir," said George shyly, twisting his cap nervously in both hands.

"Wait there," said the King's Equerry, and he walked back to the far end of the room. George watched the Equerry deferentially approach a man with a beard sitting behind a table. The remains of a meal were in front of him. That must be the King, George thought, he's a bit like his head on the coins. Then, as the man at the table half-turned, George saw that it was indeed the King.

The Equerry was speaking to the King in a low voice, and George could not hear what he was saying. Then he bowed and returned to George. "His Majesty wishes you to convey his gratitude to the Stationmaster and he will be arriving at the station very shortly."

George nodded, hardly daring to breathe for the tension he felt. He started to back away to the door, then remembered to bow in the direction of the King. The King looked amused and suddenly called out, "And to you. We are very grateful to you as well."

George gulped. "Thank – thank you, Your Majesty," he said breathlessly.

He bowed again, and again and would have kept on bowing if he had not suddenly felt himself gently propelled through the door which was then firmly shut behind him.

George let out a big, big sigh.

He ran all the way back to the station, feet hardly touching the ground and was grabbed by Mr Jellicoe as soon as he appeared on the platform. "Well?" Mr Jellicoe demanded.

George had no breath left. He heaved and panted, then

heard the sound of distant cheering. "He's here!" he managed to say then closed his eyes and took great gulps of air.

The station staff sprang into action. Fry, Holmes and Wrighton lined up smartly to attention at the side of Mr Jellicoe's old hall carpet and George joined them as soon as he felt capable of walking. Mr Jellicoe gave a last nervous twitch to straighten his own hat, then walked in a stately manner down the station platform to greet the King.

The cheering grew louder and the fireman leapt down from the front of the engine, where he had been fixing the last of the bunting. Ted Jarvis put his head out from behind the shed where he was concealed, his eyes big with excitement, and Robbie hurried across the track to join the staff.

The cheering grew louder still and suddenly there was the King, riding in a pony trap which had been hastily comandeered from the hotel. Behind him streamed crowds of children, waving Union Jacks and anything else they could find that was coloured red, white and blue.

The pony trap stopped and Mr Jellicoe bowed low, very low. The King descended from the trap and said a few words to Mr Jellicoe, who was far too overwhelmed to remember them later. Mr Jellicoe escorted His Majesty up the platform followed by the Equerry and the other men of His Majesty's household.

The group reached the carpet and the King stopped suddenly, blinked, then smiled. He exchanged fleeting glances with his Equerry then walked forward onto Mr Jellicoe's worn-out, threadbare, carpet as if he were treading the finest red carpet in the world.

Mr Jellicoe opened the door to the saloon, bowing yet again, and the King was about to climb in when he stopped, turned, stared straight at George, then waved his hand and smiled. George stared back at the King and the beginnings of a slow, satisfying smile started deep inside himself and played round the corners of his mouth.

His Majesty entered the carriage, followed by his retinue, and the door was shut. Mr Jellicoe, with all the dignity he could muster, gave the "right away" to the guard and the train smartly left the station.

Mr Jellicoe turned to George, who by now was beaming from ear to ear and, to everyone's astonishment, punched George playfully on the shoulder. "Well done, Grant. Very well done," he said.

Everyone relaxed and began to talk, but Mr Jellicoe stood silent on the platform, watching the departing train. On his face was a smile every bit as broad as George's as he pictured to himself the article that would appear in the Great Western Railway Magazine.

"Highley Station staff, under their able Stationmaster, Mr Albert Arthur Jellicoe, responded in the best traditions of the Great Western Railway Company when faced with a crisis involving no less a personage than His Majesty King Edward VII. Their prompt action proved that even the humble country stations . . ."

Oh yes, Mr Jellicoe could see it all. He sighed a sigh of pure satisfaction. His deepest ambition was satisfied at last.

One hour later, Mr Jellicoe's benign mood had gone. He had the whole station staff lined up on the platform and a full post-mortem was conducted – to the intense discomfort of Holmes and Fry. For twenty minutes, until the arrival of the 5.10, Mr Jellicoe berated everyone soundly on the unpreparedness of Highley Station to meet crises of this nature. He excelled himself, and everyone, even George, was crushed and humbled by the time the 5.10 steamed in.

After its departure, station life resumed as if nothing had ever happened.

14

The two figures were silhouetted at the top of the hill, framed by the setting sun against a golden background. George's voice floated across the field. ". . . quite fat, with a balding head and a beard."

"Doesn't sound much to write home about," said Annie deprecatingly.

"But he had twinkling eyes and – and a nice voice. And he wasn't a bit starchy or anything," George said hastily.

"I've never seen the King myself," said Annie. "Not yet. My mum has though. She said he smiled at her ever so nicely. He was on horseback or in a coach or something."

"He arrived at the station in a pony trap," said George. "They must have borrowed it from the hotel."

"Well that's not what he's used to," said Annie firmly. "Of course my mum used to live in London where the King lives, and that made it much easier."

"Yes. I suppose it does," said George, rather confused.

"She said he used to pop up all the time," Annie went on.

"I suppose I'd see quite a bit of him myself if I get a position in London."

George was quite crestfallen. Annie took his arm. "Tell me again what he said . . ." she said kindly.

George brightened. "Well, he didn't say much, not to me that is . . ." and they walked on, over the brow of the hill and out of sight.

It was quite dark when he arrived home. He found his mother and his grandfather in the kitchen having just finished their tea.

"You're very late, George," Jane said disapprovingly, removing the dirty dishes from the table.

"Yes. I . . ."

"I suppose it's that Irish girl you've become friendly with."

George blinked. He had never mentioned Annie at home and had hoped his mother did not know about her. It was not that he wanted to deceive her – it was just that he guessed that she would not approve, as she never approved of anything he did.

"It was only . . . a short walk . . ." he said lamely.

"Your grandfather has been telling me what happened at the station," Jane said, suddenly changing the subject. "He said you behaved very well and that Mr Jellicoe was very pleased with you." She paused. "I'm pleased too, George."

"Thank you Ma," said George, turning pink with pleasure. He glanced gratefully at Robbie, but his grandfather was busily engaged in lighting his pipe.

"There's some stew on the stove if it isn't all dried up by now," said Jane, and went to get it.

George sat down and his mother brought him a plate full of food. "I don't like your acquaintance with this Irish girl, George," she said. "She sounds common to me. But I suppose my opinion won't bear with you at all. You're no longer a child."

George was overwhelmed. He looked at his mother then glanced again at Robbie. His grandfather gave him a long, slow, wink.

"'Ere! Boy!"

It was a week later and the young man hailing George had just alighted from the train.

George looked round. The passenger was a self-assured young man in his early twenties, nattily dressed and sporting a boater on his head, a small moustache on his upper lip, white gloves and a cane.

"Yes sir?"

"Where's the big 'ouse eh?"

"That way." George pointed. "Just follow the lane to the top, turn right and you can't miss it."

"Ta," said the young man. He casually flicked a coin in George's direction and sauntered off.

"Grant! Come to my office," Mr Jellicoe called from the doorway.

When George entered, Mr Jellicoe was standing behind his desk, a letter in his hand.

"This has just reached me," said Mr Jellicoe. "It is a letter from Inspector Hunt apprising me of the exact train the new lad porter will be arriving on. It also confirms your promotion Grant – to Porter."

"Promotion?" gasped George.

"Mr Harvey has also been promoted. To Head Porter. Mr Holmes has been transferred to another station." He held out his hand and shook George's warmly.

"Thank you . . ." breathed George.

"You're a – a good lad Grant," was Mr Jellicoe's unexpected reply.

As soon as George was off duty he raced up the lane and turned right to the big house. He had to find Annie. He had to tell her.

"Annie!" he called. "Annie! I've been promo . . ."

He stopped suddenly, the words dying on his lips. Annie was there waiting. Annie was there, but not alone. With her was the self-assured young man and Annie was holding onto his arm. *His* Annie was smiling and laughing up at the self-assured young man and he was smiling down at her in full pride of possession. Annie looked round.

"George!" she cried. "What a surprise! I was just talking about you and how kind you'd been. I'd like you to meet Walter – my intended."

Walter slowly transferred his gaze from Annie to George. He lazily looked at George, up and down, then smiled, a mocking, arrogant smile and held out his hand. "We're already met – 'aven't we?" he said.

George, totally defeated, held out his hand.

It was one hour, two hours later. George did not know. He sat in a corner of the Great Western, a pint of untasted beer on the table while he lived and relived that agonising meeting with Annie and her "intended". He felt hot with shame and embarrassment. Then he thought back, back to every meeting he had ever had with Annie, back over everything they had talked about, everything she had said . . . the pain of it all and the humiliation were almost too much to bear.

Ted found him. He came in quietly and sat down, not speaking.

George glanced at him. "Go away."

Ted looked at him sympathetically. "I'm sorry George."

"How d'you know?"

"I'm your mate. I made it my business. It wasn't very hard though. It's a small place and news travels." He stopped and they both sat in silence.

"Come on," said Ted. "You'd better go home."

"Why . . .?" said George. "She led me on . . . never told me . . ."

"I don't know. Some girls are like that. Not all. Just some."

"Made me look such a fool . . . I know I am one but . . . her 'intended' she said. The way he looked – I could have punched him straight in the face . . . I could . . ."

"Why didn't you?"

"He was bigger than me," said George, and slumped morosely.

"Want me to?" George did not answer. "Come on mate. Home."

Ted helped George up and they went out. At the top of the lane George stopped. "I'm all right now," he said.

"I'll see you home," said Ted.

"No. Honest. I'd rather not. I don't want to go home yet. I'm all right really." George stopped. "And – thanks."

"Well . . . see you Sunday shall I? I've got this new fishing line . . ."

"Yes," said George.

Ted hovered. "Go on."

Ted punched George reassuringly and ran off. George watched him go, then wandered aimlessly round the village. He did not want to go home – he did not want to see his grandfather's concern or his mother's thinly-veiled triumph. I expect they know by now, he thought gloomily, the whole village seems to.

He wandered into the churchyard and sat on a gravestone. He had to work things out, but instead he fell to thinking about Annie's hands and her delicate prettiness.

A noise made him look up. It was his mother walking slowly among the gravestones, a small bunch of flowers in her hands. She did not see George and he watched her for a moment. He suddenly noticed that she, too, was small, and that there in the graveyard with the flowers twisting between her fingers, she looked defenceless and vulnerable.

She stopped at the foot of a grave and George went over to her. She looked up, surprised. "George!"

George did not speak and Jane seemed somehow embarrassed. "I heard about the promotion. I'm – pleased for you." There was a silence. "I was – putting these on your father's grave," Jane said at last.

George quietly took the flowers from her and laid them on the worn gravestone.

"Give me your arm George," she said, suddenly. "I'm rather tired."

He held out his arm and she leant on it. He was surprised at how frail she was and how brittle her arm felt.

"Thank you," she said and they walked out of the churchyard.

Bright and early, Highley Station staff were lined up on the platform to welcome the newest, most humble servant of the Great Western Railway.

They stood in a well-regimented row awaiting their early-morning inspection. Shoes were polished, buttons shone, uniforms were clean and pressed. Mr Jellicoe emerged from his inner sanctum with the usual harassed frown on his face. Following him was a tall, thin boy with lanky brown hair and a nervous twitch.

"Right, Roberts," said Mr Jellicoe. "Here is my staff."

He walked down the line of upright men, reciting each man's name as he passed, and Roberts followed him at a respectful distance.

"Mr Davies, Head Clerk, Mr Harvey, Head Porter, Mr Fry, Under Clerk, Mr Grant, Porter and Mr Wrighton, Shunter." Mr Jellicoe stopped. "Old Mr Grant is the Signalman and Mr Mason, our occasional drayman, is out delivering in the village. You will take your orders from myself and Mr Harvey."

He pulled out his watch. "Right gentlemen, you may go

about the Company's business. The six o'clock is almost due. Roberts, you wait here."

The engine whistled and the waiting village girls moved like a flock of chattering birds across the platform. The line of station staff broke up as everyone hurried to his post, and Harvey winked at George and nodded towards the trembling new Lad Porter.

"Carry your bags, sir," said George brightly, turning to a portly gentleman.

"I think I can carry them myself, young Grant," said the man, turning round. It was Mr Holmes who grimly climbed into the train and closed the door firmly behind him.

George gulped, but just as the "right away" had been given and the train was starting to slide out of the station, Holmes pulled the window down and poked his head out. "Good luck, Grant" he called, and the train gathered speed.

George stood and watched it go, then turned towards the pile of luggage awaiting his attention and began loading it onto his barrow.

RAILWAY
SIGNALLING

In the early days of the railways, trains were controlled by railway policemen who despatched the trains along the same piece of track one behind the other on a time interval system. As speeds increased and traffic intensified, it became clear that the system was no longer safe, as the policeman had no way of knowing whether a train had been delayed or even broken down before despatching the next.

A safer, more efficient method was devised by dividing the line into sections called "blocks". Each block was under the charge of a signalman who was in touch with the signalman on either side of him by means of a telegraph bell. The signalman controlled the trains by using mechanical semaphore signals which could be set at "danger" or "clear" by means of levers in the signalbox. If the signal arm was in a horizontal position, that meant "danger", and if it was either up or down it meant "clear". Signals which moved down for "clear" were always used on the Great Western Railway.

If a train was travelling for example from station A through station B to station C, the signalman at A would offer the train to the signalman at B. If B accepted the train, the signals would be put to "clear" and the train would proceed towards B. As soon as it entered the section between A and B the signalman at A would put his signal at "danger" to prevent another train entering the section. Meanwhile the signalman at B would offer the train to the signalman at C and would inform A as soon as the train had left the A to B section. This information would be relayed from signalbox to signalbox all the way down the line as the train moved from one block to another.

In this way trains could actually run closer together, because the signalman knew that his section was clear from his colleague who had seen the train pass.

The system worked well when two sets of rails had been laid and each track only carried trains running in one direction. But railways such as the Severn Valley had only single lines carrying traffic in both directions. At first such lines used a pilotman, one to each section travelled on each train in each direction alternately. But if the trains were not run alternately – that means two or more trains were run consecutively in the same direction – then the pilotman ended up at the wrong end of his section. The whole service was held up while he walked back to the other end where the train was waiting.

A token system was later introduced, by which a token – a metal object – replaced the pilotman. These tokens, and there might be a number of them to one section, were kept in two machines, one at each end of the section. The machines were interlocked electrically in such a way that it was impossible to have more than one token out of either of the machines at any time. Further, the signalman at each end had to depress a key before a token could be unlocked. Therefore, if a driver was in possession of one token, he would know that the others must be locked in one or other of the machines, and so no train could be coming in the opposite direction.

Later the system was made even safer by interlocking the token machines with the levers controlling the signals so that the signalman could not move the signal for a section to "clear" until he had obtained the relevant token for that section. This whole system is called the "electric train token system" and is still used on many British Rail lines today.